'It's clearly nonsense to imagine we could make something work with you living in London and me here. Now that I've met Sorcha, I know seeing her once or twice a month wouldn't be enough. Which is more than likely how it would go if we continued to live in separate countries. Our only real solution to the problem is for you and my daughter to move back here.'

'Back to Ireland?'

'Clearly, the prospect doesn't appeal to you.' Flynn could not curtail his profound dismay. But he was not about to let a second child slip out of his life so easily. Even if the prospect of fatherhood daunted him more than ever because of what had happened between him and Isabel. 'Have you forgotten who I am, Caitlin? What I can give her? Her situation would be much more secure…would you deny her a better start in life than she's got now?'

Dear Reader

In one way it's astonishing to learn that Mills & Boon is celebrating its 100th birthday, but in another it comes as no surprise! It simply proves that people will always be engaged and entranced by romance and falling in love. To love and be loved is really the essence of our human existence. Even when people act less than lovingly, at the root of their anger, unhappiness, despair, is the very human need to be accepted and loved no matter what. Just as we love our children unconditionally, I believe that adults want that more than anything else too.

Long before I became an author I avidly read romance novels, and discovering Mills and Boon® was like being let loose in the most wonderful confectionery shop and told to help myself to whatever I liked! There were so many terrific writers, telling the most wonderful stories, and not only that, they all had happy endings! Some people think that we're wearing rose-tinted spectacles if we believe in the possibility of happy ever after. My answer to that is I am personally going to keep on wearing mine if it means that I see hope and joy in the world instead of just pain and disaster.

Anyway, I hope that you will continue to read and enjoy Mills & Boon for many more years to come. I feel extremely privileged to be a part of something that has clearly brought so much pleasure to so many people for such a long time! My own contribution this month is a story set in beautiful Ireland that is personally very dear to my heart. Flynn and Caitlin have a tempestuous relationship and a difficult history, but I hope you will agree that the ties of love that bind them together are very strong…

With much love

Maggie x

THE RICH MAN'S
LOVE-CHILD

BY
MAGGIE COX

MILLS & BOON
Pure reading pleasure

First published in Great Britain 2008
Harlequin Mills & Boon Limited,
Eton House, 18-24 Paradise Road, Richmond, Surrey TW9 1SR

© Maggie Cox 2008

ISBN: 978 0 263 20227 4

Set in Times R~~oman 10½ on 12½ pt~~
07-0108-39618

Printed and bound in Great Britain
by Antony Rowe Ltd, Chippenham, Wiltshire

The day **Maggie Cox** saw the film version of *Wuthering Heights*, with a beautiful Merle Oberon and a very handsome Laurence Olivier, was the day she became hooked on romance. From that day onwards she spent a lot of time dreaming up her own romances, secretly hoping that one day she might become published and get paid for doing what she loves most! Now that her dream is being realised, she wakes up every morning and counts her blessings. She is married to a gorgeous man, and is the mother of two wonderful sons. Her two other great passions in life—besides her family and reading/writing—are music and films.

To James,
a truly kindred spirit

CHAPTER ONE

'OH, WHAT a beautiful house!'

'Yes, darling.'

'And look at the lovely horses, Mummy!'

'Yes…they're grand too.'

'Can we ride them?'

'No, sweetheart.'

'Why not?'

'Because they don't belong to us.'

Caitlin wrapped her daughter's warm palm into her own icy one and squeezed it. Outside Mick Malone's cab, which had picked them up from the airport and was taking them to her childhood home, the usually verdant but now snow-covered pastures sped past—all part of a vast country estate.

Glancing beyond the horses that were attempting to crop the frozen grass, Caitlin spied long low roofs and high hedges, and in the distance a large Georgian house, bordering on the palatial. Its long sweeping drive fanned out from a pair of massive stone pillars and black wrought-iron gates tipped with gold, and was lined with frosted conifers, sparkling in the cold January light. To a little girl raised in a cramped terraced house in a busy South London suburb Caitlin didn't doubt it must resemble something out of a fairytale, and the scene was made even more enchanting by the low orange globe setting in the west behind it.

'Who do they belong to, then?'

The child was leaning across her mother's lap to try and get a better view of the creatures that had so captivated her, her soft moss-green eyes full of hope and yet disappointment too, because she hadn't managed to procure the promise of a ride.

'They belong to a family called MacCormac.'

Her glance suddenly collided with the too-interested gaze of the florid-faced driver in front of them, and Caitlin squirmed a little in her seat as a wave of uncomfortable heat assailed her.

'I'm sure they're very nice people to have such nice horses,' the little girl chattered. 'Perhaps if we ask them ever so nicely they might let us ride them. What do you think, Mummy?'

'I think you're asking far too many questions just now, Sorcha,' Caitlin admonished her daughter, not unkindly.

Whether the MacCormac family were 'nice' people or not was hardly on her agenda right now...even if the very name was apt to deluge her stomach with wild butterflies. Not when she'd come home for the first time in four and a half years for the sole distressing purpose of attending her father's funeral.

'Kids! They drive you mad, but you wouldn't be without them,' Mick Malone cheerfully observed, determinedly catching Caitlin's eye in his mirror. 'And sure she must be a great comfort to you, now that both your parents are gone, God rest their souls.'

'Yes, she is,' Caitlin murmured, silently wishing that the man—a long-time friend of her father's—would not try and engage her in any more conversation until they pulled up in front of the small farm cottage where she'd grown up.

She was almost too weary and heartsick to talk to anyone. It simply took too much energy to respond to polite and well-meant niceties when she felt so drained and hopeless inside. *Both her parents gone…it didn't seem possible.*

Deliberately withdrawing her glance, she threaded her fingers distractedly through her daughter's fine wheaten-gold hair and prayed for the strength to deal with whatever must come in the days ahead. As well as her grief at losing her father there was another shadow looming on the horizon, and she was more than anxious at the prospect of facing it. It was one that had been weighing down on Caitlin's heart for four and a half long years, dogging her every waking moment. She was going to need all the help she could get to deal with that particular daunting spectre.

It was a throwaway remark made by one of the farmers at the local inn, while Flynn was supping his pint and wrestling with the intricacies of a legendary chieftain's battle plan for his latest book on mythological Ireland, that made him suddenly concentrate with razor-sharp acuity on the conversation being conducted at the bar.

'Tommy Burns's daughter came home for his funeral, so I hear. She was a fine-looking girl, that one…must be a grand young lady now.'

'Must have broke his heart when she took off like that. No doubt he wanted her to marry one of the local lads and stay close to home. Being as though she was his only child an all.'

'Wasn't there a rumour going round that she had a thing for that MacCormac fella? You know? The one that inherited the estate and practically half the county?'

'Aye, there was.'

Flynn froze in his seat, the blood raging so hotly inside him that he sensed sweat break out on his skin, then chill again so that he was almost shivering. He couldn't have been more shocked if he'd just heard that World War Three had been announced. Caitlin was home and her father was dead? Staring at the two thickset farmers perched on their barstools as they mutually paused in their conversation to drink their pints of Guinness—both of them clearly having no idea that he was sitting in a booth not far behind them—he grimaced and shook his head. They could not realise what a bomb they had just detonated.

Setting his own half-drunk pint down on the deeply grooved and scarred wooden table, he found that all desire to finish it had abruptly deserted him. He tugged the collar of his battered leather jacket up around his ears, then stalked from the near empty bar out into the bitter wintry afternoon. His lean face with its hollowed out cheekbones was sombrely set—as if he was preoccupied with a battle plan of his own.

As his booted feet hit the deep, impacted snow that blanketed the narrow pavement and he headed towards the corner where he'd parked the Land Rover Flynn wondered how it had not reached his ears until now that Tom Burns had died and Caitlin had returned for his funeral. Someone known to him—either family or friend—would surely have heard and told him? Nothing much went unreported in their small rural community. Was there some kind of unspoken conspiracy going on amongst the people who were close to him?

Caitlin's return had always promised to be a potential minefield after what had happened—even though he had long-ago given up hope that he might ever see her again. Certainly his family hoped he would not. The way they saw it, she came from poor farm labourers' stock and inhabited a very different world from the rich and powerful MacCormacs and their ilk... Theirs was a world that didn't willingly invite or encourage integration. They certainly hadn't been happy when Flynn had started an affair with the girl.

But Flynn had been in no mood to entertain so much as one single complaint from any of them at the time. Not from his mother, his uncles, his brother or his brother's wife...Not when he'd already buckled under familial pressure once before, when he'd been young, and had married a girl from the 'right end of the social spectrum' who'd then ended up pregnant with another man's baby while still wed to Flynn. What had sickened him the most was that he hadn't discovered that the child—a boy they'd named Danny—wasn't his until he was six months old and his wife had finally confessed to both the affair and her desire to be with her lover rather than Flynn. She'd only stayed because of the privileged lifestyle that he had been able to provide for her—apparently her lover was not quite so well off.

Devastated, Flynn had been deeply humiliated and hurt. He'd grown to care for the child. But, having no choice other than to give Isabel the freedom she'd asked for, he'd ended his travesty of a marriage and filed for divorce. But, God, how he'd missed the boy! To all intents and purposes, until he'd discovered the truth, he'd been *his son*. After that, Flynn had vowed that he would never leave himself wide open to deceit again.

It had been so refreshing to meet a girl as sweet and uncomplicated as Caitlin after that painful and bitter episode in his life. Yes, she'd been young— only eighteen at the time they'd met—but Flynn had fallen for her hard. She'd completely swept him away with her beauty and innocence…so much so that he hadn't had the slightest suspicion that she too would eventually betray him. Not with another man, but by leaving him high and dry when he'd just started to believe they might have something worth holding on to.

Flynn had never dreamed Caitlin would act so cruelly. Her feelings had always been written all over her face, and he'd had no clue that she might make such a devastating move. To be treated with such contempt by someone you were falling in love with burned worst than corrosive acid. He would have given her the sun, moon and stars if she'd stayed with him—even if he'd never got round to telling her so.

It hadn't helped his case that her father had despised him with a passion. Tom Burns had never hidden his dislike. He'd scorned Flynn at every turn, even once telling him that he wasn't good enough for his daughter and who did Flynn think he was using his position to take advantage of her? Flynn didn't doubt that Tom had encouraged Caitlin to leave. It was clear that her father's continual besmirching of Flynn's character had influenced her in the end. So she'd left, and Tom had refused point-blank to tell Flynn where she'd gone. In contrast, Flynn's family had breathed a collective sigh of relief at the news...

Reaching the snow-laden Land Rover, Flynn imagined his blood pressure rising to dangerous levels if he didn't soon have some outlet for the rage that was brewing inside him.

Caitlin was home again. The pain jack-knifing through his taut hard middle almost doubled him in two. It might have been only yesterday she'd walked out, instead of almost four and a half years ago. *Wasn't time meant to be the great healer?* What a joke that had turned out to be! Jamming his key into the lock of the driver's door, he cursed the air blue as, in his haste to turn it, his numbed fingers slipped and he almost ripped off a thumbnail.

It was two days after her father had been buried when Caitlin first set eyes on Flynn again. She'd sensed his gaze on her long before she'd turned in the street and had her intuition confirmed.

Leaving Sorcha at home with a kindly neighbour who had offered to sit with her for a while, she'd come into town for some groceries, welcoming the chance to have a few moments to herself outside all the grief and sadness that lingered back at the cottage. It felt like cloying ghostly cobwebs clinging to her very skin. Her progress from shop to shop had been unexpectedly impeded—not just because of the snow that dictated she walk more slowly, but because she'd found herself stopped every now and then by people offering condolences. It seemed that she hadn't been forgotten, even though she'd moved away.

And then there had been that intense warning prickle at the back of her neck that had alerted her to the fact she was being watched. Her heart jolted hard against her ribs as she moved her head to the side and saw Flynn MacCormac, standing there on the other side of the street. For a moment the whole world seemed to turn on its head, and then in a split second was transformed by complete and utter stillness…as if everything around her was holding its breath.

A small gasp—a sound only Caitlin heard—eased out slowly from between her lips. Straight away she detected a disconcerting change in him. Not a physical one, but one more psychologically rooted. Her intuition told her that he'd closed in on himself even more than before, and the knowledge sent her stomach plunging to her boots. It was as though an impenetrable glass wall now isolated him and his feelings firmly away from the rest of the world.

He'd ever been reclusive—keeping his deeper emotions and thoughts mostly hidden and resisting anyone getting too close—but he was so beautiful he was like a burning flame to a moth. His very presence elicited excitement and a forbidden sense of danger too. Tears burned in Caitlin's eyes, and although the fabric of them was deeply sewn with unbreakable threads of sorrow for what she had lost, they were also shot through with a fierce, almost violent joy at seeing him again.

She barely moved as he crossed the road to join her—a tall, broad-shouldered figure, dressed from head to foot in black, moving with the predatory, almost feral grace of a creature. She couldn't take her eyes off him…

'I heard you were back.' His voice sounded slightly rough—as though some unexpected emotion had partially locked his throat.

Caitlin's own mouth was so dry she could barely get a word past its arid landscape. His jade thick-lashed eyes were intense and hungry. 'My father died…I came home for the funeral.'

His hard jaw seemed to tighten, but there were no immediate condolences forthcoming. She hadn't expected there would be. He would have nothing good to say about her father, and although it grieved her she couldn't really blame him.

'So I see,' he said instead, and then, before Caitlin could reply, 'I won't ask how you've been keeping because you look well enough…but you might tell me where you've been living all this time?'

She put a shaky gloveless hand up to her straight blonde hair and the edge of her palm glanced against her cheek. Right at that moment she was convinced that there was not a scrap of difference in the temperature of her skin and the hard-packed ice covering the pavement.

'London…I've been living in London. With my aunt.'

'That's where you went when you left?'

Beneath his harsh, accusing glare, Caitlin felt like the worst criminal in the world. 'That's right.'

'So you didn't fall ill, get abducted by aliens or lose your memory?'

'What?'

'How the hell would I know what happened, seeing as though you never even thought to tell me you were going?'

She flinched as though he'd slapped her hard. It took her a few moments to recover. 'Must we discuss this in the street? If you want to talk, I'll talk…but not here.'

Glancing across Flynn's broad shoulder, Caitlin's blue eyes briefly scanned the snow-covered street that was dotted with mid-morning shoppers. She felt suddenly intensely vulnerable. She'd already discovered that there were people here who knew her, and some of them had no doubt heard about what had happened between her and Flynn. The idea that people were watching them made her skin crawl. All the odds had been stacked against their relationship from the outset. Nobody had wanted them to be together, and nearly everyone had disapproved. *But none of that would have mattered if Flynn had truly let Caitlin into his heart…and if she had allowed herself to fully trust him…*

'Tell me something. Would you have come to see me at all if I hadn't bumped into you like this?' he demanded.

'I was intending to do so…yes.'

'I wonder when that would have been, Caitlin? After all, you must have such a busy life…so busy that you couldn't even pick up the phone and ring me! Not even *once* in four and a half years!'

'I know it must have seemed heartless what I did, but—'

'Heartless?' he mocked. 'Sweetheart, that doesn't even come close!'

'What I mean is—' She faltered, her heart going wild. 'You obviously want an explanation, and you have every right to one, but this is hardly the right time or place, Flynn.' Knowing that her eyes must convey at least some of the tremendous guilt that was churning her up inside, Caitlin frowned. 'We haven't seen each other for years, and believe me—

I deeply regret that everything went so wrong in the end.'

'Do you?' Flynn's glance was unflinching in its raw intensity. 'And why did it go wrong, Caitlin? I'll tell you why! Because you ran away! You ran away without even having the damn decency to tell me why!'

Shivering, Caitlin lowered her gaze. What could she tell him? He no doubt believed that it had been her father who had influenced her decision to leave and end the relationship. God knew Tom Burns had made his dislike of Flynn and his family only too clear. His antagonism had gone deeper than mere dislike...he had actively resented the MacCormacs with a vengeance—despising their wealth and the influence they had in the community. But if Caitlin's only hurdle in being with Flynn had been her father's temper and his aversion to the match she could have got over it. She'd loved Flynn with all her heart. He had become as essential to her as her own breath. But she hadn't left him because of her father...It had been much more complicated than that.

There'd been that humiliating conversation she'd overheard between Flynn and his mother, during which Estelle MacCormac had been so un-stintingly cruel in her summation of Caitlin's motives for seeing her son. *'She's only sleeping with you for what you can do for her and that dreadful father of hers! Don't kid yourself that a girl like that cares a fig about you personally! Next thing you know she'll be trying to trap you into marriage by telling you that she's pregnant!'*

Hearing herself spoken about as if she were the most awful little trickster, Caitlin had reeled away in shock and horror. After that, coupled with her father accusing her of bringing 'shame and disgrace' on him, by behaving like a little slut with Flynn MacCormac of all people,' she'd had no choice but to phone her aunt Marie in London and ask if she could go and stay there for a while. Especially as she had also just found out that she was indeed pregnant with Flynn's baby…

It would have done no good trying to talk to him and explain. He would hardly have been likely to believe anything she'd said after his mother had done her worst. And, although Flynn had passionately demonstrated that he wanted to be with her, he'd never actually said that he loved her. In fact he'd hardly ever opened up to her about his personal feelings at all. Consequently Caitlin had found herself unable to trust him with her doubts and fears. So, instead of screwing up her courage and confronting him, she had fled to London.

She hadn't meant to make it a permanent move, but time had overtaken her and, consumed by her new parental responsibilities, she had had no choice but to stay and try and make the best of it. Every day she'd been away from her homeland…away from Flynn…her heart had grown heavier. But how could she ever have gone back when her news might only have confirmed to him his mother's belief in her motives? She'd had no choice but to let him go.

As the years had passed and she'd made a life for herself and Sorcha it had grown ever harder for Caitlin to contemplate returning home. She'd always known Flynn must despise her by now, and she'd been heartbroken at the thought of facing his contempt…as she was facing it right now. And he didn't even know about the child they had made together yet…

'So, what is it you want to do now, Flynn?' Her heavy sigh made a plume of steam as it hit the near freezing air, and Caitlin at last lifted her gaze to face him again. The formidable chill in his glance had not lessened any.

'What is it I want to do?' His green eyes narrowed to icy slits. 'You know what I'd *like* to do? I'd like to cross back over the road the way I came and pretend I hadn't seen you! Why couldn't you have just stayed in London and not cursed me with the sight of you again? Why did you have to come back at all?'

She'd never heard him sound so frighteningly bitter. His tongue lashed her like a whip, almost cutting her knees from under her and making her shake. Her blue eyes watered alarmingly.

'My father died…I told you. I only came back for the funeral.'

'I want to talk to you. I want to talk to you, and it had better be soon! You're damn right you owe me an explanation, and I'm not letting you run away from me again without it!' Letting out a harsh breath, as though every word he'd uttered had caused him some considerable pain, Flynn raked her from head to foot with his burning stare, as though daring her to even *think* of defying him.

'The standing stones at the top of Maiden's Hill.' Her voice sounded as if it had been dragged through gravel. 'I'll meet you there tomorrow afternoon at three. I want to sort through some of my father's belongings in the morning and decide where they're going to go.'

'Three it is, then. And, Caitlin?'

Her heart slammed like a wrecking ball against her ribs at the look he was wearing. 'Yes?'

'Don't let me down. If you do…I'll come and find you.'

And with that he left her there on the pavement, her legs shaking so hard and her heart beating so fast that she couldn't move for several minutes, until she had calmed down sufficiently again to think what she was doing. By which time she was numb with cold and desperately in need of some warmth.

Seeing the little blue and yellow sign above Mrs

O'Callaghan's bakery swinging back and forth in the wind, Caitlin headed over there—to the prospect of a steaming mug of milky coffee to help thaw the chill and the *dread* from her bones.

CHAPTER TWO

CAITLIN arrived at the standing stones early, bundled up warmly in corduroy jeans and a chunky knitted sweater beneath her coat, to stave off the relentless slicing wind that was already making her face burn with cold. Standing on the edge of the ridge with the stone circle behind her—all six-feet-high shale stones erect, apart from one recumbent in the middle—she stared out at the stormy Irish Sea, smashing wildly onto the rocks hundreds of feet below, and sensed a small flame of pleasure light inside her. It was a breathtaking location, and one she'd often yearned to go back to when she was far away in the busy traffic-jammed streets of London.

A magical haunt, with or without the numerous legends that surrounded it, it had taken on an extra enchanting quality after many times spent there with Flynn. They had even made love there one warm midsummer's night, with the moon's shining face showering them with its silvery light…as if it approved of their being there together.

Her blood throbbed with a primitive and powerful need at the recollection. Perhaps it hadn't been such a good idea after all that this be the place they meet? There were too many memories that lingered here…stirring, soul-ringing memories of love that were only taunting shadows of a path not taken. And now Flynn wanted answers…answers that behoved Caitlin to tell him that she'd had a child, and that *he* was the father.

She knew exactly the moment he arrived, because there was a frisson of electricity running through the air that made her scalp tingle in alert. It was ever thus that she had been so psychically attuned to his presence. As if they'd had some strange other worldly bond that mysteriously linked them together.

Wrenching her hypnotised gaze from the commanding sight of the foaming white-capped sea below her, Caitlin turned and saw his masculine dark figure striding towards her over the brow of the hill. The savage wind that was swiftly gathering force was now accompanied by spots of sleet that flattened his clothing against his lean hard body and turned his gleaming black hair to wet silk. Her violent shiver wasn't just because of the icy cold that seemed to penetrate her own clothing and lay its death-like fingers on her bare flesh. A powerful swathe of want and need throbbed through her, and—too swept up in its passionate grip to move—she remained where she stood, a prisoner to its force, nervously watching him approach.

'You came.'

Flynn didn't smile as he released the words that were swiftly borne away on the soughing wind. Instead, he stared at her like a man possessed by a dream. Sleet clung to his ebony lashes and made the fascinating jade of his remarkable eyes glitter like flawless gemstones.

'It's bitter.' Her teeth chattering and her boots shifting on the slippery frost beneath her, Caitlin wrenched her gaze free from his unsettling, diverting glance and started to move past him. 'It's a day for staying by the fire…not freezing to death!'

'Let's go over by the stones,' he sombrely suggested. 'It might shelter us a bit.'

Trying to brush back the windblown hair from her face, Caitlin glanced up into his solemn visage as she stood with her back to one of the standing stones, its dark companions making up a loose enclosure around them. Closely observing the way the taut skin stretched over his hollowed-out cheekbones, she saw how it rendered the implacable bones of his jawline rigid as iron. There was no spare flesh there. None. Its stark and fascinating definition could have emerged out of granite or marble, it was so faultlessly constructed. There was a fair smattering of dark growth shadowing the mainly smooth surface, though it was likely he had probably shaved only that morning, and his face reflected an austere and sombre beauty that seemed to come from the earth herself. It was no wonder that he seemed to blend so well into this wild and rugged landscape.

While Caitlin was so earnestly examining him, Flynn wasted no time in doing the same to her. Her chest tightened as she became weakly, stunningly aware of the raw need that was reflected back at her. To be observed in such a primal, voracious way by him snatched the breath from her lungs, made her feel as if she was drowning in a sensual aquamarine sea that commanded the total surrender of all her senses.

'We'd better get this over with,' she heard herself say, and there was an emotional catch in her voice as her hand moved to restrain the dancing wheat-coloured strands of hair that the wind was buffeting around her frozen face.

She realised in that moment the devastating extent to which she had missed him. As though Flynn was the absent part of her soul that she'd always ached for—a silent, hurting emptiness that never diminished. Only Sorcha had made her life worth living again since she couldn't be with him.

'Why?' he murmured gruffly as his hands

dropped loosely to his hips. Then, before she could answer, *'Why?'* with all the primitive force of a glacier splitting open. His expression was savage.

Flynn's heart was pounding with more force than a blacksmith's hammer as he searched Caitlin's shocked white face for an answer. Did she have any idea of the wasteland of misery and pain she had consigned him to when she'd left? Did she know how it felt to have every day of your life since feel as if it were a hundred years long? Without love, without warmth. Winter, spring, summer and autumn—all had turned into one long, never-ending season of darkness and unhappiness.

Only his work gave him any solace. His writing career had really taken off after Caitlin had left—but then how could it not have when he'd made it his sole driven focus? His dedication to learning his craft, to improving and refining the books that had university professors and television producers alike clamouring for him either to lecture or make programmes about Ireland's Celtic mythological legacy, had become vitally important to his psychological survival, and took up a large proportion of his time. But other than that time hung about like stale cobwebs in an empty, long-disused room.

Flynn had good people to help him run Oak Grove—the impressive MacCormac estate—and it had not been that difficult for him to pursue his chosen career. Even though his family still believed that looking after the estate should be more than enough…

Now, as he considered the brilliant sapphire-blue eyes and the beguilingly shaped lips before him, he realised that no matter how much his heart was secretly thrilled to see Caitlin again forgiveness would be no easy matter after what she had done. There was no excuse on earth that he would accept for her deserting him like that. *None.* And that included her father persuading or bullying her into break off their relationship, people gossiping about them, and the difficulties they'd faced in trying to be together in the face of their families' hostility to the idea. Clearly, whatever feelings Caitlin had harboured for him, they hadn't been strong enough to persuade her to stay.

Flynn knew his shortcomings where relationships were concerned, and he was quite aware that he wasn't an easy man to love or to be with. Hadn't Isabel already proved that? He could be both taciturn and morose, and the tendency to both had worsened after his ex-wife had so sorely deceived him. But when he'd met Caitlin he had started to hope that the trust Isabel had violated might one day be tenderly reinstated. But it was not to be…

In search of the peace of mind that so eluded him, Flynn had renovated an ancient cottage in the mountains and turned it into a writing retreat. Pretty soon it had turned into a retreat *per se*. It was simply easier *not* to be around people sometimes, and it helped to have a place to escape to. Once upon a time Caitlin had managed to come somewhere close to penetrating the hard shell he'd built around himself, but when she'd gone he had strengthened it doubly.

Now—and not for the first time in all the years they'd been apart—Flynn mused on whether he had imagined her tenderness and affection towards him. Could her seeming attraction for him have been just a product of a young girl's fickle nature? An attraction for an experienced older man that had been there one minute and gone the next? What if she'd had a better offer of a more tantalising future somewhere else, and she'd been unable to resist and couldn't bring herself to tell him? Was *that* why she had left?

Flynn deliberately slowed his breathing in a bid to calm himself down, even though his hands had clenched into fists of bitter frustration by his sides.

'My reasons aren't—they aren't easy to explain,' she said now, reluctantly answering his question.

The wind tore at her lovely yellow hair, and Flynn longed to grab a handful of its spun silk and submerge his senses in the wild, rain-washed scent of it. He intimately knew her body's perfume, and time had not dulled it in his mind. But his fury hadn't abated, and he clung onto its force to ground him, to try and kill the almost painful desire that was surging through his bloodstream just because he was near her.

'I've got all the time in the world, darling,'' he mocked, his glance hard and impervious as the standing stones that encircled them. 'If it means we stand here and freeze to death until I get a satisfactory answer then…so be it.'

'Well, I don't want to stand here and freeze to death!' Caitlin retorted with some spirit. 'I want to get home. I have a lot to do to sort my father's house out before I go back to London, and there's only me to do it!'

'So you're going back to London?' he ground out through gritted teeth. 'I suppose you can't wait to leave? Once upon a time you said you wouldn't want to live anywhere else in the world but here…that you loved the landscape, the weather and the wildness…that it was in your *soul*. Clearly the temptations of London held far more allure for what I now know to be your true fickle nature, Caitlin.'

'I'm not fickle! And I still love it here! In London it's hard to breathe sometimes…too many people, wall-to-wall traffic and everyone on a treadmill they can't get off! If it's got a soul at all I never came close to finding it…not in all the time I was there. Not like this place.'

'But the fact still remains that something lured you there!' Flynn shook his head, still fighting to hold onto his temper. 'What was it? Another man?'

'No!' She looked aghast, the gusting wind turning her corn-coloured hair into a gilded fan across her face. She pushed it impatiently away. 'How could that have been possible? I spent all my spare time with you, Flynn! I only wanted to be with you!'

'You're lying. You must be! You forgot this place—this land you purport to love so much—as easily as you forgot me!'

'I didn't forget you. I never—' She stopped, her expression bleak.

Fighting a dangerously treacherous urge to hold her, Flynn deliberately took a step back—as if afraid his body would act of its own volition without his strict and guarded control.

'Nobody wanted us to be together, Flynn... Can you remember how difficult it was?' Her voice was too soft, and he almost had to strain to hear the words beneath the howling of the wind. 'My father...your family...they kept trying to keep us apart.'

'Not good enough, sweetheart. Try again.'

'I was only eighteen! What could I do? I had no power, no say in anything! And it was always per-fectly obvious that your family wanted you to be with someone much more suitable, from your own class and background, not some farm labourer's daughter like me! Did you think I wanted to hang around and eventually see that happen? I know I should have told you that we should finish and that I was going away, but—but when it came down to it I just couldn't face you. You probably think I'm a terrible coward, but everything was just getting me down back then. Including the way my dad was with me.'

'You should have *told* me that! Not left me in the dark about how you felt!'

'It wasn't so easy for me to talk to you about personal things back then.'

'Why not?'

She looked as if she was struggling to answer him, and Flynn sensed the tension inside him build almost to the point of pain.

'You—I didn't think you'd understand. You always seemed so impervious to feelings. I was afraid you'd just try to brush my fears off…tell me not to be so stupid.'

'I'd never have done that!' He was genuinely shocked.

'I'm just telling you how I felt.'

'If you'd done that four and a half years ago, instead of just walking away like you did…out of the blue and without warning…we might have been able to salvage something out of the situation. Instead you left me with nothing, Caitlin! *Nothing!* And then to have your father gloat in my face that you'd finally come to your senses and realised you were better off elsewhere! A place he had no intention of giving me the location of! *That* I can neither understand or forgive!'

'I—what can I say except that I'm very sorry? Sorrier than I can ever begin to tell you.'

Touching her hand to the large standing stone at her back, it seemed as if she was lost in some melancholic memory Flynn couldn't share. He fought like a Trojan to keep the urge to shake her at bay, even as the scent of the sea filled his nostrils and more sleet settled in his hair.

'So that's it? That's all the explanation I'm going to get?'

'It's—it's freezing out here. We ought to go—'

'Didn't you hear what I just said?'

This time he completely failed to keep his frustration at bay. It didn't seem enough somehow, what she'd told him. Surely there had to be something else to complete the puzzle of her desertion? And what did she mean by him seeming so impervious to feelings? Dear God! It was his *feelings* that had damn near crippled him these past few years with her gone!

But in the end Flynn knew that whatever embellishment Caitlin might come up with none of it would make him feel one damn bit better. He should accept that something about him hadn't been enough to hold her and just forget her. Get on with his life as he had been doing until she had so unfortunately returned for her father's funeral.

Now the chill in his bones was nothing to do with the sharp-bladed cruelty of the weather. It was just too bitter to see her again and watch her walk away a second time...

Staring at Flynn, at the dismay and disappointment etched into the haunting lines of his face as though they might take up permanent residence there, Caitlin didn't have the courage to just come out and tell him about Sorcha…the beautiful child they had made together. She was frightened of how he would react, and was undone by the thought of him hating her worse than he must do already for her desertion. To learn that she'd had his baby and had kept the news from him for all these years would be far too devastating a blow for him on top of having to deal with her unexpected return.

It had stunned her to consider that he'd cared for her to such a degree that he was still furious at her leaving. The Flynn she remembered had not been a man who had readily or easily revealed much about what he was feeling. Except when he was making love to her… Then there had been no barriers to stop him from showing her exactly how he felt. Sometimes, alone in her bed at night in London, Caitlin had no difficulty in conjuring up the thrilling memories of how this man had loved her, and it had kept her warm even when she'd felt as if her heart was rent in two for ever.

There was no doubt she would have to tell him about Sorcha some time soon. But it just couldn't be right now.

'I know we have unfinished business, and there are things that I should say…things I should have told you before I left. Maybe when you've calmed down we can—'

'Calmed down?'

She could see that wouldn't be happening any time soon. She exhaled a resigned sigh into the frigid air. 'I can see you're still mad at me, but maybe that's why we should both have some time to think things through before we meet again?'

'Think things through? What the hell do you think I've been doing for these past four and a half years?'

He took a step towards her, put his face up close to hers—so close she could see every tiny grooved line and pore indenting his skin. She could see the midnight shadow that studded his well-defined jaw, and Caitlin's heart thudded in shock at the barely contained anger that rolled off him towards her.

'I thought—' She took a nervous swallow. 'I thought you might have married again or—or perhaps be living with someone by now?'

Oh, how she'd dreaded that. Even though there was no earthly or logical reason why Flynn shouldn't be with someone else by now.

'I'm no celibate priest, but I'm not in a relationship, no. Why, Caitlin? Did it make it easier for you all these years living in London to think of me being with someone else? Sorry to disappoint you. I guess betrayal leaves a nasty taste in the mouth that's not easy to relinquish. These days I have only one real use for women, and I'm sure you don't need me to go into details!'

'No, I don't.'

It was almost more than she could bear to imagine him for even one second with another woman, doing the things he had done with her. *Oh, God…would this pain ever heal? This longing for him abate?* Fixated on the beautiful sensual mouth that hovered so near, Caitlin could almost taste the kiss that her lips longed for. His kisses had been heaven and forbidden fruit all at the same time. Her knees went weak as water at the memory.

As if not trusting himself to be so close to her, Flynn moved abruptly away again—but not before his jade eyes made a blistering examination of her face.

'And what about you, Caitlin? Do you honestly mean to tell me that there's been no other man in your life since you left? That you've spent every night in your bed alone?'

'It doesn't matter what I say, does it? You'll believe whatever you want to believe!'

'Can you blame me?'

He strode right away from her then, driving his hand in mute outrage through his sleet-sodden black hair.

'Flynn!'

She ran after him, cold to the bone and shivering uncontrollably.

'Please don't just walk away!'

'Why not?' he growled, his expression bleak. 'Isn't that what *you* do?'

'Please, Flynn,' she implored again, too weary in mind, body and spirit to argue any more—knowing whatever she said would likely be a red flag to a bull while he was in this frame of mind. 'I don't want us to be enemies. I know we can't be friends, but don't you think we could try and resolve our differences and at least be civil to each other?'

'We'd better get out of here.'

Ignoring her plaintive question, Flynn pulled up his jacket collar as far as it would go, with freezing hands almost blue with cold. In spite of his animosity and anger towards her, he could see that Caitlin was in even worse straits. Her wheaten-gold hair was drenched and flattened to her head, and her lips were almost colourless…like wax. The last thing she needed after just burying her father was to come down with a bout of flu…or even…pneumonia.

'This wind is getting worse and the light is going. Did you make your way here by yourself?'

'I got a lift to the road and walked from there,' she replied, her teeth chattering.

'My Land Rover's parked down at the bottom. I'll run you home.'

For a moment she looked as if she might refuse

the offer of a lift, but a second later she briefly inclined her head.

'Thanks… Just halfway down the lane will do. I can walk the rest of the way from there.'

When Flynn pulled up in the lane that led to what had been Tom Burns' old cottage, he switched off the ignition and turned in his seat to regard his now silent passenger.

'We could meet at the house tomorrow at around ten. Do you want me to come and get you?'

'No, it's all right. I prefer to walk. Ten it is, then.'

She pushed open the door at her side and stepped down onto the snowy road without another word.

Flynn sat and watched her walk up the lane—a slender, duffle-coated figure with bright hair whipped by the wind—and he gripped the steering wheel as though he would break it, shuddering out a long, slow breath.

CHAPTER THREE

SHIVERING, Caitlin wrapped her arms around her chest to try and retain some warmth inside. Since returning from Maiden's Hill with Flynn she had hardly been able to get warm at all. It was as though some of the ice and snow that covered the beautiful, haunting Irish landscape had seeped into her very bones...drip by freezing drip. Knowing she was finally going to have to tell him about Sorcha tomorrow, she fleetingly mused on how his family would react to the news that the girl they'd so looked down their noses at had a child by Flynn. No doubt they'd instantly believe that she'd come home to try and trap him—just as his mother Estelle had once told him she might.

With her daughter tucked up safely in the old iron-framed bed she had slept in as a child, Caitlin stared out through the back door of the small farm cottage into the inky darkness of the freezing night, lifting her gaze to the sprinkling of bright stars that were like a glittering breast-plate above.

None of them burned with the same intense flame or hue as Flynn MacCormac's unforgettable eyes… And today those same eyes had regarded Caitlin with fury and loathing in their depths for what he clearly perceived as her careless and thoughtless desertion. It was so unfair! And why should all the blame fall on *her*? If only he had been more emotionally giving and less remote some-times, she might have been able to open up to him as she'd wanted. How could she have told him she was carrying his child when she'd had no clue at all as to how he might react to such momentous news? What if Flynn had believed that Caitlin really *was* some conniving little gold-digger, out to try and trap him into a commitment he didn't want or desire? Such a destroying assumption would have made a complete mockery of her love for him…a love that she had known to be pure and true.

Her throat tightened painfully when she remem-bered how hard she'd cried on that plane journey across the sea to London—far from her home…far from the man she loved.

When Flynn found out about Sorcha she knew his heart would probably petrify against her com-pletely…that it was likely he would never forgive her. How would she live with that? Especially if he wanted regular contact with Sorcha from now on?

How would she cope if he wanted his child but viewed her mother as somehow not good enough or trustworthy enough to be associated with his illustrious family? Her humiliation at the hands of the MacCormac clan would then be complete…

Returning from his early-morning ride on the stunning grey mare he had recently purchased from an elite stables in Dublin, Flynn left the horse in the capable hands of his top stable-hand, with instructions to get her dry and warm as quickly as possible and give her a feed. Then he went back to the house for a quick hot shower and a change of clothes before Caitlin arrived.

The elegant Georgian mansion he had lived in from a child contained four different wings, each with its own self-contained living quarters. But now Flynn was the only one who lived there. Although, truth to tell, he spent more time these days up in the remote cottage he'd renovated. After Isabel had done her worst, he had more or less viewed the big house as a place in which to conduct the business of the estate and little else. He took no pleasure in its timeless elegant beauty, and found himself brooding far too much when he was there. When Caitlin had run out on him he'd almost come to despise the place. It was as though all the vast rooms and corridors mocked his unhappy inability to turn it into anything close to a home…a home with a wife and children and all the comforting paraphernalia that came with having a family.

Danny's nursery was empty and cold, and Flynn had finally locked it up—unable to bear even glancing at the door that led into the room where his little boy had slept.

Now, today, after a mostly sleepless night spent thinking about Caitlin's visit, he was irritable and on edge. That was why he'd had to get out of the house early and expend some energy with a brisk ride in the hills. The glacial air had chased away most of the fogginess in his head and the tiredness in his limbs, and now his body was thrumming with renewed purpose and anticipation. He probably shouldn't be giving Caitlin the time of day after the way she'd treated him, but she'd hooked him by telling him there were things she should have told him when she'd left, and he couldn't help but be intrigued.

And somewhere in amongst his feverish thoughts was her accusation that he had been 'impervious' to feelings. It had prompted a curiously defensive reaction in him, because he intuited that her statement skirted too close to the truth. He knew he would have to maintain his usual rigid guard throughout their encounter. The force of Flynn's attraction for Caitlin hadn't diminished over the years…it had simply been lying dormant, like a silent but ever-flowing and forceful river.

Having showered and combed his hair, he wrapped a towel round his lean, hard middle and crossed the huge high-ceilinged bathroom to the marble vanity unit on the other side. Squaring his jaw, he stood in front of the gilded antique mirror, preparing to shave. Seeing the ridiculous gleam of hope and excitement flaring in his green eyes, he turned impatiently away to mutter a harshly voiced oath…

Caitlin had visited Flynn's private quarters at Oak Grove before, of course, but it intimidated her no less to visit the grand, imposing house again. Standing in his elegant sitting room, with a good fire blazing in the exquisite fireplace, surrounded by gracious, comfortable furniture and with fine paintings adorning the walls—each no doubt valuable beyond belief—she felt a little like Alice in Wonderland after she'd drunk the potion that had rendered her so impossibly small.

The contrast between his wealthy background and the impoverished one of her personal humble beginnings had never stared back at her with such clarity. Thinking of her father's damp, rundown cottage all but brought tears to her eyes. Then, quickly remembering that she had nothing to be ashamed of—she'd come from staunch, hard-working stock—Caitlin lifted her chin a little and declined Flynn's less than warm invitation to sit down.

'I won't stay long,' she asserted, her blue eyes

nervously arresting on his sombre face. 'I'm busy sorting out some of my dad's things to give to the church for their next jumble sale. Not that there's a lot to give. He wasn't one for acquiring material things. There was only himself after I went, and as long as he could listen to the racing on the radio and buy himself a pint now and again he was happy.'

Was that true? Caitlin's stomach seemed to plunge to her boots at the realisation that she hardly knew if her father had been happy or not. He had had too much anger and resentment in him to be happy. After her mother had died, she had rarely seen him even smile.

'Come and stand near the fire.' Moving towards her, Flynn intensified his gaze. 'You're shivering.'

'I'm all right.' Her lips trembled on a little half-smile, but the gesture was quickly gone again as Flynn drew level with her. Now she experienced a different kind of intimidation. Her awareness of his daunting masculinity and strength almost robbed her of the power to speak...especially knowing what she had yet to reveal to him.

'You're not coming down with a chill after yesterday?' he demanded, his expression surprisingly concerned.

'No...no, I'm not. Flynn, I—'

'You cut your hair.' His voice had lowered to the hypnotic nap of luxurious velvet, and Caitlin sensed her whole body tighten in exquisite response.

'It's more practical for work to wear it short. Easier to manage,' she murmured. 'I see you've grown yours.'

He was staring at her and didn't look away. 'I'm viewed as quite the bohemian these days.'

'You always went your own way, as far as I could tell.'

'You didn't seem to mind.'

'I liked it that you were…different.'

'So, tell me…do you still have a penchant for older men, or have your tastes changed since you've been in London?'

'That was unnecessary!'

To Caitlin's consternation Flynn reached out and touched her hair, completely immune to her discomfort at his definitely barbed comment. Her heart went wild as he drew his palm over its softness.

'What do you do in London, by the way?'

'Do? I—I work in a bookstore.'

She saw an interested gleam in his aquamarine gaze. Yes, she knew about his books—and she had thrilled to see them, to see his photograph on the inside jacket sleeve. For a while it had given Caitlin the confirmation she'd yearned for. He still inhabited the world safely. He was now a much-admired author and clearly doing well.

Her breathing became shallow. His hand still brushed against her hair, and was sending little flashes of disconcerting electricity up and down her spine. *He should stop it. He should stop it now, before she had no will left to summon for her protection.*

'You're a writer now yourself, I see? They sell your books in the store. I got—I got quite a shock. I knew you wrote a bit, but you never told me you intended to write books. Your family must be very proud.'

'Proud that I haven't made Oak Grove and all its doings my one and only passion?' He wryly moved his head. 'I don't think so. Besides…I don't see them much these days.'

Lifting his hand from her hair, he positioned his fingers beneath her chin instead. His warm breath skimmed over her, and although his skin smelled mainly of soap and aftershave, she detected the arresting scent of snow-covered hills and valleys and sweet fresh air too. Flynn was a true Celt, both in heritage and in spirit. He simply worshipped nature in all its myriad forms, and loved nothing better than to be outside, breathing it all in—whether that meant strolling, hiking or riding through the countryside, or simply being at one with the beauty of it when watching a sunrise or a sunset. There wasn't a house in all creation that could contain that restless spirit of his. No wonder he'd chosen Celtic mythology as the subject for his books.

'What are you doing?' Caitlin asked—aware that

everything in her had tightened in exhilarating anticipation as he lowered his dark head to hers.

He didn't reply to her question, simply breathed out on an impatient sigh and then boldly took what he was so anxious to savour, touching his lips avidly to hers.

At the first pulse-racing contact her spine seemed to turn to mush, and protesting against his embrace was not even in her mind. Instead, her hands reached out to rest on his waist, in a bid to balance herself as he impelled her hard against his chest. His objective was to angle his kiss even more intimately, and as his tongue thrust hotly into her mouth his fingers pressed hard into her back, to try and obliterate any sense of separation between their two bodies at all…to make them as one.

Four and a half years ago a kiss like this would have had only one destination, and both of them would have moved heaven and earth to get there. But now, as the memory of her daughter waiting at home with a neighbour for her return stole suddenly into Caitlin's brain, reminding her of the real reason she was here—not to make love with Flynn, but to tell him that he'd fathered a child—she started to pull urgently out of his ardent embrace.

His frustration was immediately evident in the harsh-sounding breath he expelled, and the slightly dazed look in his darkened jade eyes. His lips twisted wryly.

'I would apologise,' he asserted mockingly, 'but I'm only human—and you do seem to have this inconvenient ability to raise my temperature at the drop of a hat. Given what's happened between us, I should learn to resist it better.'

'We should talk about the reason I'm here,' Caitlin announced abruptly, striving to sound confident when all her senses were still under siege from his sexy, knee-trembling kiss.

Hugging her arms over her chest in the soft dove-grey sweater that she wore with her jeans, she found herself moving nervously across the room towards the fire. As the flames spat and crackled and hissed round the logs she stared at the fiery dance, silently searching for the right approach...the best way to break the news. News that would stop his world and change its pattern for ever... *Or maybe it wouldn't?* In the end she knew that there was no correct protocol or any sensitive couching of words to soften the blow—she simply had to state what it was and leave it with him to do with the information as he may.

'I have a child—' she began—and, intimately attuned to every nuance and gesture he made, she easily sensed his immediate confusion and shock.

'A child?' he echoed.

'Yes. A little girl... Her name is Sorcha.'

'Well, now...' Nodding his head, Flynn more than adequately reflected the derisive bitterness of that one telling phrase in his tone. 'So you didn't lack for male company in London after all? Of course you didn't! What normal red-blooded male could resist a girl who radiates innocence and sex in the same seductive package as you do?'

'I've never slept with any other man but you, Flynn.' Her expression was in earnest. '*You're* Sorcha's father…no other.'

'Good God, woman! You must think me the biggest fool that ever lived!'

His words were like the score of a sharpened blade across her heart. She sensed the wound gape open even before he'd finished speaking.

'Of course I don't think that! And I'm not trying to treat you like one either! I'd never deceive you about such an important thing. *Never!* I'm not interested in playing those kind of cruel, manipulative games. I know you may think that I've left it a little late, but I only want to try and put things right…to set the record straight. I realised when I was coming back for the funeral that it was time you found out the truth about what happened after I left. Sorcha is nearly four. I've got her birth certificate with me if you want to see it and the date is self-evident.'

At first he couldn't believe it was happening to him again. That another woman was declaring him the father of her child and expecting him to unquestioningly accept it as fact—as though he lacked even the most basic capacity to discern truth from falsehood.

It was several seconds before Flynn could see past the red mist that seemed to rise up and blur his vision. It had been bad enough when Isabel had lied to him about the child she'd carried being his. Especially when he'd found himself growing to love little Danny and making the discovery that he actually *welcomed* becoming a father. He'd known that the marriage itself probably wasn't destined to last—but then how could it have been when he'd been all but 'coerced' into the relationship by his parents? Yet he would have worked hard to make the union work if the child had truly been his and not some other man's. What cut deep was that somehow Flynn had always expected better and more from Caitlin. He'd honestly believed she was incapable of acting wilfully in anything. *Until she'd left him, that was...*

'If she's my child, as you say she is, why didn't you contact me before now?' he demanded furiously, hardly knowing how he contained his rage. 'And what if your father hadn't died? Would you have even bothered to let me know about her at all?'

'I—I didn't contact you before because I didn't know how you'd take the news. You were always such an enigma to me, Flynn...I never knew what you were thinking from one moment to the next! You rarely shared your private thoughts with me. How could I know that you'd even *want* a child? When we were together you never expressed whether you thought our relationship would lead anywhere or not. I just thought—I just thought you believed it was an affair we were having...something that would sooner or later come to an end. And I didn't want you to be with me just because I fell pregnant with your baby.'

'So instead of even giving me an opportunity to say what I wanted, you ran away?'

She hung her head and stared at the floor. 'You make it sound as though the decision was easy for me.'

'Well, clearly you overcame any scruples you might have had and left anyway!'

'Don't, Flynn!'

'You're seriously telling me I have a child, and that she's nearly four years old?'

'Yes.'

Her lip quivered, but Flynn ignored the tears that he saw glistening in her eyes. If this latest experience with women's deceiving ways didn't scar him for life, he didn't know what would!

'And you've raised her by yourself during all these years? There's been no other man involved?'

'No!' Her expression was wounded. 'My aunt Marie helped me to raise her. She looked after Sorcha for me and I had to find a job to support us.'

'I must be in the middle of some kind of nightmare!'

'Please don't say that! Is it so terrible to learn that you're a father?'

Danny's cherubic face hoved into view in Flynn's anguished mind, and the pain that accompanied the picture was indescribable. Swallowing hard, he strove to recover his bearings.

'And where is she now? The child, I mean?'

'Back at the cottage. A neighbour is sitting with her while I've come here…Mary Hogan.'

'Mother of God!'

He turned away then, allowing a reluctant acknowledgement that she might—just might—possibly be telling him the truth. He might be the father of a little girl he had never seen—a child who was nearly four years old.

He definitely hadn't always been as scrupulous about contraception as he might have been, he guiltily recalled. There had been times when his passion for the woman who now stood before him had broken all its bounds and pure wild feeling had had its untrammelled way instead. He had started to let down his guard a little with Caitlin…had started to trust her. He had never guessed that she would desert him as she had.

There were hardly words to describe what he felt right now. Shock, disbelief, soul shattering astonishment… Nothing could come close to conveying the fierce tumult of emotion that rocked through him.

'I'm sorry.'

Her words were so soft Flynn barely heard them.

But they made him turn back to face her just the same. The heat from the fire that blazed behind her had tinted her smooth pale cheeks to a healthy rosy glow, and her gold hair gleamed with the sheen of a polished blade—as though she stood beneath direct sunlight. Even now—even when his life had been thrown into profound chaos by what Caitlin had told him—his body blazed with an unholy fire for her. Yet he had to fight the attraction. Because there was a hell of a lot at stake here…not least a child's future, as well as Flynn's sanity.

'Sorry, is it?' he mouthed harshly, shaking his head. 'Such a small word to convey what must be no less than your complete and utter *contempt* for me! All I can say is that you'd better not be lying to me! If you are then by God you'll be the one who's sorry, believe me!'

'You don't need to threaten me. Why don't you come back with me now and meet Sorcha for yourself? She has a look of you about her, even though her colouring is fair like mine.'

'You've told her about me?'

Flynn hardly knew what to think about that. The pain of losing Danny had made him fear loving another child ever again. Was he even capable of such a thing when it felt as if his very heart was wrapped inside a steel cage these days? Yet he couldn't deny there was a strong sense of anticipation and excitement flowing through his veins too—

even though he was bitterly angry that Caitlin had deliberately kept this momentous revelation from him.

'I haven't told her. No. I didn't know what you'd want to do, so I thought it best not to say anything until you'd reached a decision. I can tell her you're a friend, if you like? Perhaps that would be best for now.'

'Best for whom?'

'There's no point in telling her you're her father if you decide you don't want anything to do with her…that's all I meant. It would be too upsetting for her and she wouldn't understand. She's only a baby.'

'If I *am* her father—' a muscle ticked clearly in the side of Flynn's smooth-shaven jaw '—then I want her to *know* that I'm her father. There's to be no more pretence or lies. God knows, I've had my fill of lies to last me a lifetime!'

'I hear you.'

Her small chin went up then, as if to show him she was not intimidated either by his threats or his temper, and a part of him secretly admired her courage. Even though he was in no mood to be conciliatory after what she had just revealed.

'I'll get my jacket, then we'll go.'

He walked to the door, leaving her to quickly collect her duffle coat from the chair he'd laid it over and hurry after him.

When Caitlin and Flynn arrived back at the cottage Sorcha was sitting at the small table in the parlour with Mary Hogan, poring over the thick, generous-sized pieces of a puzzle they were doing together.

Immediately self-conscious about the poor decorative condition of the tiny cramped dwelling—its only bright point the blazing fire that burned in the grate—Caitlin couldn't help but see what had once been her home with Flynn's no doubt highly critical gaze. After the opulence of Oak Grove, this cottage must seem like very mean fare indeed. The chairs around the table were roughly hewn and old as the hills, and the rest of the sparse furniture looked about ready for chopping up into firewood. The stone floor had but one faded rug to adorn it, and was hardly conducive to making the room warm and welcoming.

Swallowing down her embarrassment, and sure that all Flynn's attention would naturally be on the little girl who was his daughter anyway, Caitlin smiled at the diminutive Mary Hogan, thinking that the woman must be in shock at seeing one of the illustrious MacCormacs walk into the room.

Although he was wearing just a plain dark sweater and jeans beneath his three-quarter-length black leather jacket, the sheer quality of his clothing and his handsome looks easily set him apart from most of the folk who lived in that small rural community. And that was *without* the knowledge that his family practically owned everything and anything worth having in the area. There was even a mountain named after them, for goodness' sake!

'Hi, Mary. I've brought home a visitor, as you can see. This is Flynn MacCormac. Flynn, this is my father's neighbour—Mary Hogan.'

'Mary.'

Flynn courteously shook the elderly woman's hand, but his gaze moved from her almost immediately to alight on the small elfin-faced child who was presently assessing him with a stare that was openly curious.

'And this must be Sorcha?'

She knew she hadn't imagined the slight break in his deeply resonant voice. Caitlin wondered if Mary had heard it too, and what on earth the woman must make of it all. Luckily for her, her dad's gentle neighbour wasn't an inveterate gossip, like some. She took a deep breath to steady herself.

'Sorcha, darling…say hello to Flynn.'

'Hello.'

The little girl's thumb was immediately inserted into her mouth after her shyly voiced response, and her small hand slipped swiftly into her mother's, seeking reassurance. Caitlin tenderly ruffled the silky blonde hair.

'It's all right, sweetheart. He might look fearsome, but he won't bite you!'

Desperately seeking humour to decrease the

tension, she glanced nervously up at the man standing by her side, and saw to her relief that there was a definite flicker of a smile touching his otherwise stern mouth.

'I only bite when I'm very, very hungry,' he teased. 'And, luckily for you, I had a big breakfast before I came out this morning!'

'Now, who would like a nice cup of tea? Mary?'

'No, thanks, Caitlin dear. I'll be getting along home now, if you don't need me for anything else. Now you've got company. I'll pop round in the morning before I go to the shops…see if you want anything then. And don't forget the casserole I've left in the oven for you and the little one. You can have it for your tea.'

Stooping to collect the large dyed cloth bag in which she kept her knitting and two sets of spectacles, Mary moved towards the parlour door.

'Thanks a million, Mary…you're a godsend! And thanks for taking care of Sorcha for me this morning too.'

'My pleasure. She's a grand little girl, so she is! Your father often used to show me her picture…he was so proud!'

Catching Flynn's eye as she turned towards him, Caitlin sensed a shiver of unease go through her. He was no doubt furious that Tom Burns had kept the news from him that he was the father of his daughter's child. She just prayed he wouldn't give rein to his temper while Sorcha was there. It wouldn't be a good beginning for the child to see them arguing.

'Nice meeting you, Mr MacCormac! I'll see myself out, Caitlin. You go on inside and be with your visitor.'

'Mind you go careful back down the lane. That ice is treacherous!'

'Don't worry about me. I'll take my time, so I will.'

When Caitlin stepped back into the parlour, Flynn was sitting in the chair Mary had vacated, talking softly to Sorcha. At the sight of her daughter's bright hair and her father's midnight-dark locks leaning towards each other over the slowly forming picture puzzle, her heart almost lost its rhythm. They looked so right, sitting together like that, and Caitlin couldn't help but feel profoundly guilty that it was she who had kept them apart all these years.

'I'll have that cup of tea now—if you're still offering?' His implacable jade glance briefly touched hers before swiftly returning to Sorcha and the jigsaw. 'Now...I'll bet you any money that this little fellow slots in here... See! What did I tell you?'

'You're right!' Sorcha exclaimed in delight, clapping her hands together.

As emotion swelled inside her throat, Caitlin turned hurriedly away into the kitchen to make the tea...

CHAPTER FOUR

CAITLIN couldn't ignore the fact that after Flynn's initial good humour around Sorcha a definite awkwardness and reticence had seemed to steal into his manner. It was as though he were deliberately holding himself emotionally apart from his child— as if he didn't trust that she was *indeed* his daughter.

It had been a fraught couple of hours, with Caitlin doing her level best to cover the tension-filled gaps in conversation and Sorcha regarding her mother's visitor extra-warily…as if she too sensed his discomfort with her. At first Caitlin had thought Flynn would stay just a short while and then quickly leave. He'd clearly need time to take in the news that he was now a father. But, in spite of his withdrawn manner, he'd surprised her by seeming in no hurry to go at all.

After making them lunch, and then settling Sorcha down on the threadbare couch with a blanket tucked round her for her afternoon nap,

Caitlin felt she could finally talk to Flynn more freely.

'We're leaving in a few days, and I wondered if you'd decided what you want to do about seeing Sorcha again?'

Her voice had a tremor in it, and she really wished it didn't.

Taking up the too-small old-fashioned armchair with his impressive physique, his long legs stuck out towards the now simmering fire, Flynn studied her for several long seconds before replying.

'You were right about her looks,' he said. 'There's definitely a family resemblance. The MacCormac genes are strong.'

Caitlin found herself holding her breath. She folded her hands in her lap and waited.

'I can't believe your father knew all this time that you'd had my child and deliberately kept it from me! I used to see him from time to time in the town, and he always walked past me without saying a word, or looked right through me as if I didn't exist. And people think the MacCormacs are arrogant!'

'He was only acting out of concern for me. You were—you were who you are, and an older man. He believed you were taking advantage of me. He was only protecting me, that's all.'

'But to keep your whereabouts from me, and the fact that you were carrying my baby a secret! If he were still alive I'd— Never mind! It's just unbelievable he did what he did. Surely it must have crossed his mind that I'd want to see the child, have some part in her upbringing, for God's sake? No doubt he concluded that I didn't *deserve* to know.'

He'd raised his voice, and Caitlin glanced anxiously towards Sorcha on the couch. But the little girl went on sleeping peacefully, her plump round cheeks flushed from the heat of the fire.

'I don't know what he thought—except that he was furious with me when I told him I was pregnant. He accused me of bringing great shame on him. He was very old-fashioned about things like sex before marriage…his strict Catholic upbringing, I suppose. Anyway…we rarely made contact after I left to go to England. I sent him letters, photos of Sorcha, but he didn't often reply. I was totally shocked when Mary said he'd often shown her Sorcha's picture and indicated how proud he was of her! She might just have said that to be kind, though.'

Pulling her troubled gaze away from his too-intense examination of her, Caitlin linked her hands awkwardly together in her lap.

'I'll want to have access now that I've seen her, of course.'

'Are you sure, Flynn? You seem—you seem hesitant. It must be a great shock to you to learn that you're a father. I understand it might take time for the reality to sink in.'

'You have no idea *what* I'm feeling!' he came back, jaw clenched tight.

'Then tell me!' Caitlin implored, blue eyes glistening. 'At least then we might get somewhere! You must know that I would never try and force you into doing anything you didn't want to do. Even acknowledging that Sorcha is yours!'

He seemed to mentally regroup, as though he regretted his telling outburst. 'I want you both to come to my place in the mountains tomorrow. We can continue this conversation there. Right now I have to go and prepare some work to take with me.'

He pushed to his feet, his imposing height and broad shoulders relegating the already small room to doll's house proportions.

'You bought that old cottage in the mountains?' In spite of her sorrow that Flynn obviously couldn't trust her with the truth about his feelings, Caitlin felt his comment pique her interest.

She stood up beside him, all of a sudden remembering that he'd taken her there once, to show her the dilapidated dwelling that the estate agent had drolly referred to in its advertising blurb as 'a pile of stones with a resident goat'.

Flynn allowed himself a smile. She'd been utterly charmed by the place, seeing all kinds of whimsical possibilities in the rundown building *and* the goat.

'I not only bought it, but I had it completely renovated too.'

'Really? How wonderful! And that's where you write your books?'

'It is.'

'You can't lack for inspiration, then. You'd have to go far to find a more spectacular location!'

For a moment Flynn forgot to be mad at her—forgot that she'd walked out and kept her pregnancy from him—and in place of his anger a rogue arrow of warmth and affection helplessly pierced his heart. Perversely, once upon a time the only peace he'd ever really known had been with Caitlin. Her innocence and joy in the simple things of life had accorded him great pleasure. But that had been a long time ago, and a lot of turbulent water had flowed under the bridge since then...

'That's true enough.'

'And what about the goat? What happened to him?' she asked.

'I donated him to a local farmer.'

'You should have kept him. He was a real character.'

Feeling oddly chastised, Flynn firmed his mouth.

'I'll come and pick you up around one. Make sure you're ready and wrapped up warmly, the both of you. It'll be a bit of an arduous journey in this arctic weather, so it's just as well to be prepared. I'll see myself out. Until tomorrow, then.'

He went out through the front door before he

caved into the powerful urge to pull her into his arms. It wouldn't be the wisest of moves, under the circumstances. He surely needed to keep a clear head to think through all that had happened.

Braving the wind and sleet with his head down, Flynn negotiated the icy pathway to his vehicle with his mind focused astonishingly on the fact that he was a father now, and would once again have to learn how to be around a child…to maybe care for her, when to do so would make him risk his heart in a way he'd never thought to do ever again.

The following day, when the time came, Caitlin honestly couldn't attest to how her legs carried her towards the waiting Land Rover at the end of the lane. She'd crossed the first major hurdle, in telling Flynn he was a father, but she didn't doubt there'd be many more challenging obstacles to come. She was entering into the realm of the unknown and she couldn't help but fear it.

A thought had crossed her mind last night that, when he'd mentioned access with regard to Sorcha, had Flynn possibly been referring to a joint custody scenario? It was a prospect that filled her with trepidation for several reasons—not least that they lived in two different countries. It might mean longer separations from her daughter than Caitlin could tolerate…

Beside her now, her daughter's normally cheerful chatter had stilled to an apprehensive silence that tugged at her heart, and the little girl gripped her mother's hand with uncommon tightness.

'You know the man you just met?' Caitlin had told her yesterday, when she'd woken from her nap. 'I have to tell you, darling, that he's your daddy.'

Sorcha's soft green gaze had mirrored her innocent confusion straight away. 'Really?' she'd asked, her voice falling to a captivated whisper. 'I didn't know I had a real daddy!'

'Well, you do, sweetheart. It's just that when Mummy had you, we weren't together.'

'So Flynn—the man that helped me with my puzzle—is my daddy?'

'Flynn MacCormac…yes.'

'The same name of the people who own the lovely horses?' Sorcha had excitedly exclaimed.

'That's right,' Caitlin had answered, the inside of her throat feeling scratchy as sandpaper.

'But, Mummy…what if he doesn't want a little girl like me?' the child had responded, her smooth brow puckering. 'He waited such a long time to come and see me! Why did he, Mummy? Why did he wait so long?'

Caitlin had had to glance quickly away then, to hide her tears…

The snow covered the hedgerows in a glittering white shawl as they made their way up the lane, their booted feet gingerly negotiating the hard icy surface beneath them.

Flynn's practical Land Rover was one of the only all-terrain vehicles that had a chance in this seriously inclement weather which closed roads and made frustrated motorists abandon their cars. It would be the only possible means—apart from hiking or helicopter—with which to reach the secluded mountain cottage he'd purchased.

Caitlin had loved its remote location as soon as she'd set eyes on it. It was a wild, mystical place, surrounded by areas of concentrated woodland full of ancient oaks that made a patchwork of the sky and held a silence where you could hear every beat of your own heart as well as the sound of your thoughts. And not far away was a clear path to the top of a mountain peak from which there was the grandest view of the majestic sea, in all its myriad hues: aquamarine, duck-egg blue, misty grey and mossy green. That view would ease the sorest of hearts…

Yes…Caitlin knew intimately why Flynn had been unable to resist the chance of having a refuge in such a place. If a man sought any kind of peace or solace away from the world then he would surely find it there.

Up ahead, he'd stepped out of the driver's seat and stood watching them as they approached—a dark imposing figure that even from a distance seemed to convey command. Caitlin felt the power of his searching gaze—first on herself, then on their child. What was he thinking? Would he be examining that sweet elfin face with those soft innocent eyes that held traces of both her blue and his jade colour in their fair-lashed depths, to ascertain that she was really his? Would he still hold the possibility in his mind that Sorcha might be another man's child after all? Her heart lurched as they drew level.

'Hello,' she greeted him, her lips moving in an uncertain smile. He didn't answer her. Nor did he smile. Instead he stooped down low, so that he was level with the little girl standing quietly at Caitlin's side, her hand still holding on tightly to her mother's.

'Hello, Sorcha,' he said gently, gravely. 'It's nice to see you again.'

'Hello,' the child replied quietly, stealing a glance upwards at her mother before returning her gaze solemnly to Flynn. 'Did you know that I'll be four years old on my next birthday?'

'I did know that. Sure, that's a great age, isn't it?'

His smile was clearly in evidence now, and the dark beauty of it was purely breathtaking in its effects.

'Are we going to your house now? The one with the horses?' Sorcha asked, her voice sounding undeniably hopeful.

'Horses?' Flynn glanced up at Caitlin and frowned.

'She saw the big house on the way here from the airport,' she explained, sensing hot colour rush into her face. 'She asked me who owned the horses in the paddock and I told her it was your family.'

'I see.'

He rose to his full height again, and his hand glanced gently against the top of Sorcha's woolly indigo-coloured hat. 'I'll take you there to see the horses very soon,' he promised, 'but right now I'm going to take you to see my house up in the mountains. It's quite a long way to go, so I think we'll get in the car, shall we? It's not good to stand around for too long in this perishing cold.'

'Take off your coats,' Flynn instructed, serious-faced, as they entered the rustic-styled porch of his secluded mountain home. 'I'll put the under-floor heating on but we can have a real fire too—if you'd like?'

'That would be nice,' Caitlin agreed, surprised he'd consulted her on her opinion.

He'd hardly spoken a word on the treacherous journey to get there, no doubt sensibly preferring to concentrate his well-honed driving skills on getting up the narrow mountain passes safely. Behind him, Caitlin had sat quietly, with Sorcha snuggled deep into her side, her wary sapphire-blue gaze often resting on the back of Flynn's dark head, as well as on the sheer drops they skirted so breathtakingly close to.

The tension produced by the dangerous conditions of their journey, coupled with the unspoken strain that lay between them, had felt as heavy as a dragoon's thick dark cloak, enveloping them all, and Caitlin had longed for something light-hearted or diverting to ease things a bit. But now at last they'd arrived, and the scene that greeted them was like a winter wonderland illustration from a child's book of fairytales—low roofs at the centre of mountainous white peaks and frosted treetops. Her heart lifted at being back—in spite of the tensions of the journey.

Although the renovations Flynn had made to the ancient stone cottage and its various outbuildings had been by necessity quite major—to make it habitable and also to bring it up to modern-day standards—Caitlin knew he had a preference for the natural heat that came from glowing turf fires and, in the less inclement weather, sunlight. Consequently she'd intuited that the interiors would also be sympathetic to the cottage's stunning surroundings, and reflect as much as possible a natural environment.

As she and Sorcha followed Flynn's tall figure into the comfortable living room, with its wood-panelled flooring, attractive muted-toned rugs and huge open-plan windows at the back of the far wall, which seemed to invite the snow-covered landscape inside, Caitlin found she wasn't disappointed. And as he stalked over to the wide stone hearth, with its carved wooden mantelpiece, crouching low to light the already made-up fire in the grate, her senses were swamped by memories.

He had done this for her before…lit a fire so that they could talk, eat and make love with the dancing flames warming them on a cold day just like today…Her heart skipped a beat when she saw the poignant selection of seashells positioned on a little walnut table next to the window. She was certain they'd collected them together on one of their long walks on the beach. And there on the wall were the four simple prints of the mountain view in spring, summer, autumn and winter, which Caitlin had bought Flynn for his birthday. They would have looked entirely out of place in his grand apartment at Oak Grove, with its valuable antiques and paintings, but here they were just perfect. She was inexplicably touched that he'd put them here, in the place where he retreated from the rest of the world to write…a place he had brought Caitlin to see before anyone else, because she had instinctively known what it would mean to him.

She frowned as she stooped to undo the buttons on Sorcha's light-coloured sheepskin jacket and remove her gloves.

'There you go, angel!' Snapping out of her reverie, she grinned lovingly at her child, her hand ruffling the waving golden hair that fell about the small shoulders as she lifted off her woolly hat and stood up straight again.

Immediately she sensed Flynn's watchful eyes on them both. 'I expect the pair of you could do with a drink?'

Rising from the hearth, where the fire had started to crackle nicely, he dusted down his black cord jeans with his hands. There was so much they needed to discuss—but how to accomplish it with Sorcha so close by?

Caitlin's nerves bit with frustration and tension. 'Why don't you let me put the kettle on?' she suggested, inserting a falsely cheerful note into her voice that was a feat in itself, given the strained circumstances. 'You could talk to Sorcha on your own for a bit, if you like?'

She was trying to make peace, of sorts. Hard in view of the threats he had issued yesterday, and what he might yet demand regarding parental access, but she had to try for her daughter's sake.

'Sure. The kitchen is just to your right there. You should easily find everything you need, but shout out if there's something you can't.'

'I will.'

Her automatic smile had all the effect of water glancing off a duck's back. His sombre expression didn't change one iota. He seemed to be brewing a lot of resentment towards her today. No doubt time to think had only increased it.

Caitlin willed herself to try and relax. 'I'll go and make some tea, then.'

'There's some fresh juice for Sorcha.'

'Great.'

In the large bright kitchen—traditionally the hub of Irish family life in these old cottages—Caitlin had no trouble in locating the makings of a pot of tea. Everything was in beautiful order, and was indeed easy to find.

As she watched the kettle start to steam on one of the iron plates of the beautifully restored old-fashioned range she heard muted conversation coming from the living room with bated breath—Flynn's velvet rich tones and Sorcha's answering softly childish one. She knew she couldn't hold back the tide now that her secret was out, but she feared for the backlash she might come under from Flynn's family when they heard the news. That was, if they hadn't heard it already.

'You found everything?'

Suddenly Flynn came through the doorway, his tall, broad-shouldered presence in his dark clothing seeming to dominate the room—for it was impossible to look anywhere else when he was near.

'Yes, thanks… What you've had done with this place is amazing! It's beautiful, Flynn,' she added warmly, pouring boiling water onto the leaves in the ceramic teapot.

He ran his gaze over her curves in the light blue

sweater she wore with her jeans, and for a long moment silence stretched ominously between them. Caitlin tried in vain to keep her hand steady as she continued to pour the water.

'It was definitely a labour of love,' he finally admitted, again surprising her with the admission.

'I can see that.'

'She's so bright… Her vocabulary for a child so young is quite extraordinary.'

The unexpected comment elicited a burst of warmth inside her, and Caitlin looked straight at him. It was a shock to see the depth of emotion written there in the compelling planes and angles of his darkly riveting features.

'Yes. She picks things up very quickly. She's also got a will of iron, and can be a right little madam when the mood is on her, so don't be fooled altogether by that "butter wouldn't melt" expression!'

'Like her mother, then?'

The softly spoken remark sent goosebumps chasing over the smooth surface of Caitlin's skin.

'You said you had some juice?' she mumbled.

'In the fridge. There are some biscuits in the cupboard too.'

'We can't leave it too late to get home. Those roads were treacherous, and you shouldn't be driving them in the dark.'

'Anxious to leave already, Caitlin?' A muscle

visibly throbbed under the skin of one shadowed cheekbone.

'Not at all!' She coloured as she put the tea things on a nearby tray, to carry them back into the living room. 'I know there's a lot we still have to discuss.'

'An understatement, if ever there was one.'

Throwing her a glance that drove away the previous warmth she'd felt, he turned and went back to rejoin his daughter.

While Sorcha was stretched out on the rug in front of the fire, drawing in one of his unused sketchpads with some crayons Flynn had found for her, he moved his gaze to her mother, sitting on the far side of him. She was sipping her tea and staring into the flickering blue and yellow flames as though transfixed. The reflection of the fire's warmth turned her hair into a rippling stream of gold and he couldn't help but secretly admire it.

It was hard to believe she was back. If he closed his eyes and opened them again would she disappear altogether? If she did it would be proof that she was just a figment of his fevered imagination—because this place had lost some of its meaning for him since the day she'd left, no matter how much a labour of love it had been, or how beautifully it had been transformed. He sighed, and Caitlin immediately transferred her gaze from the fire to him.

Studying the serene face, with its smooth untroubled brow and shimmering china-blue glance, Flynn sensed a bolt of despair pulse through him. Why had she treated him with such contempt by keeping Sorcha's existence a secret? He still couldn't understand it, no matter how hard he tried.

'Where is the bookshop you work at in London?' he asked, grasping a neutral subject out of the sky and willing the fire in the pit of his stomach to abate—because he wouldn't lose his temper in front of the child and risk frightening her.

'Just off Tottenham Court Road…it's quite a well-known one. You can get practically any book you want there.'

'And does this aunt of yours know that you were intending telling me about Sorcha at last? What's her opinion of the whole debacle?'

He knew he was glaring, and he saw Caitlin pull her glance awkwardly away for a moment at his swift change of subject, as if to garner her defences.

'We did discuss my telling you…and she was, of course, anxious.'

'I'll bet she was,' he replied, low-voiced and grim, and saw her flinch. 'Seeing as she must have colluded with your father all these years to keep your whereabouts and the fact that you'd had my baby a secret.'

'She advised me to try and heal the past the best I could by telling you the truth.' Leaning forward with her hands in her lap, Caitlin implored him with her eyes. 'Aunt Marie didn't condone my father's behaviour *or* mine. But she helped me because we're family, and she loves me.'

'And did either one of you spare *me* so much as a thought, while you kept me from my child as you did?'

Inevitably his voice—underscored by emotion—had grown louder, and Sorcha glanced up at him gravely from the picture she'd been so busy with.

'I want to build a snowman!' she declared, and in the next moment was scrambling to her feet and planting herself in front of Flynn, small arms akimbo. She didn't look dissimilar to some seriously ticked-off schoolteacher, confronting her wayward class. 'You *have* to help me!'

Surprise and pleasure swiftly acted as a salve to the anger that had seized him, and Flynn stood up and held out his hand to the little girl. 'It's been years since I've built a snowman, darlin'. You'll have to show me how.'

'Don't worry,' Sorcha replied confidently, smiling as she slipped her small pale hand into his. 'I will!'

'Don't forget your coat and hat and gloves, Sorcha Burns!' Caitlin called, and twisted round on the couch to watch them as father and daughter headed off towards the front porch.

Stopping for a moment to glance back at her,

Flynn let her know with the hardening of his gaze in no uncertain terms what he felt about his daughter not having *his* name. When Caitlin's cheeks coloured softly, he knew a certain grim satisfaction that his unspoken disapproval had hit its target.

CHAPTER FIVE

THE snowman was a resounding success—even if Flynn said so himself. His daughter seemed delighted with the results, at any rate. She was a robust little thing, he thought with unexpected pride, watching her clap her hands together with glee as she stared up at their handiwork beside him, even though her gloves were soaked through and she must be frozen to the bone.

She'd worked hard and without complaint, piling handfuls of snow upon snow as Flynn had strived valiantly to fashion some sort of recognisable snowman shape out of the powdery ice. He was out of practice with this sort of thing…*years* out of practice. That was the trouble. There hadn't been many children in his life at all since his own childhood. And because that had been a somewhat solitary one, in spite of his brother Daire—who'd had his own set of friends and scorned his big brother's company whenever he could—Flynn had not found a lot of pleasure in childish pursuits. Apart from reading and going off into the woods on expeditions of the imagination.

All the same, he'd derived a fierce enjoyment from meeting his daughter's passionately voiced request. They'd finished the large rotund figure off by inserting a pair of coals for eyes, a withered carrot for a nose, and wrapping a striped woollen scarf round the solid wide neck. After adding a smiley face with his finger, at Sorcha's eager instigation, the job was done. And now Caitlin stood in the doorway of the porch to assess the results of their labours, her arms folded against the raw wind that swirled fresh flakes of snow everywhere and her face wreathed in an admiring smile.

'He's fantastic, isn't he? A real character! Well done, both of you!'

In a totally unguarded moment Flynn got swept up in the radiance and warmth of that smile, and to his alarm found himself reciprocating. Then, in the next instant, he remembered the suffering she'd caused him and the gesture was withdrawn as swiftly and emphatically as though it had never been.

'Better get her inside and warm her up,' he murmured, putting his hand between Sorcha's small shoulders and guiding her towards the porch.

'I'm going to call my snowman Tom, after my grandad!' the child announced proudly as she climbed up the steps towards her mother.

'That's a grand idea,' Caitlin agreed, wrenching her wary gaze away from what Flynn knew was the less than animated expression on his face.

Personally, he neither wanted nor needed any reminders of the man who had played a part in driving Caitlin away from him, and thereby depriving Flynn of his child. As Caitlin turned away towards the living room, and the fire he guessed she would have kept blazing to warm them on their return, Flynn moved past her to go into the kitchen.

'I'll make her some hot chocolate while you get her warm again. There's a blanket in the box at the side of the couch—you should wrap her up in it.'

'Thanks…I will.'

Her expression even more guarded now, and her smile banished, Caitlin continued on into the living room.

With growing anxiety she had watched the cold day's short span of light rapidly fade outside the windows, as the fire she'd tended continued to throw off its glowing welcome heat into the room. On the comfortably upholstered sofa beside her Sorcha had fallen into a deeply tired doze, her little body worn out by the afternoon's strenuous snowman-building and by the relaxation encouraged by the big mug of milky hot chocolate Flynn had made her. She was wrapped in the luxuriously soft tartan blanket that he had urged Caitlin to use, and only the child's small pink-cheeked face and spun-gold hair showed above the blue, red and green checked wool as she sank ever deeper into a more contented rest.

They would have to leave soon if they were going to get home at all tonight, Caitlin thought worriedly, her glance flicking once again to the windows and the dusk that was descending outside, along with more snow. It would be madness to attempt the drive back down the mountain in near darkness.

Flynn had left them alone for quite a while now, but she knew he was in the kitchen preparing food by the delicious scents that were wafting through the cottage, making her tummy rumble with hunger. But, hungry or not, she would have to insist they left directly.

Just as Caitlin decided she would have to go and tell Flynn so, he came back into the room, his gaze falling at once upon the sleeping child, her feet stretched out on her mother's lap and her golden head resting on a multicoloured cushion.

'I thought that might happen,' he commented, moving towards the fire and tending it with the poker that lay on the hearth in front of it. Little orange sparks flew up at the disturbance, and settled again to make the flames dance higher and brighter.

'She couldn't fight it any longer.'

Pursing her lips before continuing, Caitlin felt her heart flutter wildly at the sight of that strong, resolute profile of his, and the way his well-defined thigh muscles had stretched the fabric of his jeans as he crouched before the fire. The flickering light from the blaze made his handsome visage an almost intimidating bronze mask, and at that moment she wondered if she'd imagined all the times she'd been able to coax him out of a black mood and make him smile. *Never again...* Never again would the power to do that for him lie with her. It was like waking up one morning and learning that there would be no more spring, only winter for ever.

'Flynn, I think we'd better get—'

'Remember what the Celts called this time of the year?' he asked, turning his dark green glance towards her.

How am I expected to remember anything when you look at me like that? Caitlin thought frantically, as her body was suddenly stormed by hot licking waves of intimate heat.

'No...no, I don't.'

'*Anagantios*...stay-home time.'

'I suppose it makes sense. What else would you really want to do in this weather if you had the choice?'

He'd always shared his love of the Celtic way of life with her. In fact it had been her own interest in

the folklore and wisdom of her ancestors that had
led her to the library in town to hear Flynn talk
about the major Celtic feasts and festivals one soft
rainy night just five years ago. Enthralled beyond
words by both the man and the talk, she'd shyly
sought him out afterwards, amid a queue of others
waiting to ask questions. The fact that he was a
MacCormac, and an educated, cultured man with
a sharp intelligence that could be intimidating,
should have given her pause—but she'd managed
to put aside her apprehension and speak to him
anyway.

One thing had led to another when their gazes
had locked for that very first time, and neither of
them had been able to readily look away from the
other. Before she'd returned home that night Flynn
had invited her to join him the next evening for a
drink. Caitlin had known her father would likely
want to kill her when he found out—but what she'd
experienced when she'd set eyes on Flynn that very
first time no threat or lock and key devised could
have prevented. She could still recall the passionate, intense excitement of it all, and the astounding
revelation that love really could happen at first
sight.

'You and Sorcha are going to have to stay the
night. Obviously I shouldn't attempt the drive back
down the mountain in these conditions tonight.
Besides…it's been snowing heavily again.'

Getting to his feet, Flynn laid the poker carefully back down on the hearth. Now Caitlin's heart really did pound in alarm.

'We can't stay the night! You know we can't!'

'Why?' His lips twisted with derision. 'Do you think I might try to get you into my bed again? Do you think I have no pride left after what you did to me? Don't worry, Caitlin…as irresistible as you are, I do have some scruples left, even if you don't!'

Admonishment blazed in his eyes, enough to ignite her where she sat, and Caitlin was submerged by a cloak of the utmost desolation. She'd killed what little trust he'd begun to extend to her when they were together completely with her actions…even though they'd been committed under duress, as well as in the inexperience of her youth.

'I'm sorry. I'm sorry I hurt you so badly that you can never forgive me.' She swallowed across the lump that seemed to swell and burn inside her throat. 'But you hurt me too, Flynn. I know you can't see that, but you did. You shut me out emotionally and made it hard for me to get close to you. I don't understand why, when I made it pretty obvious that I was mad about you! But there… What's done is done, and we can't turn back the clock. I know we had something special, and that I smashed it all to dust when I left without telling you. I've had to live with that knowledge every day! Every time I look at Sorcha and see your likeness in her eyes, in her smile… Every time she reaches another milestone in her childhood and you're not there to witness it… Don't you think I think of what I've done and regret it? Regret it with every breath in my body?'

'Yet you clearly didn't regret it enough to come back and face me with the truth!'

There was not a flicker of compassion or forgiveness in Flynn's chilling glance, and Caitlin saw to her frightening cost that her initial summation when she'd seen him in town the other day had been right. He'd closed himself up so tight against any future possibility of hurt or slight that there was no getting through the iron wall of his defence. Not even a battering ram could make a dent in that impenetrable armour of his.

'You and Sorcha can sleep down here.' He shuddered out a long breath. 'It's the warmest room in the house. That other sofa opens up into a bed. I'll bring down some bedding later. In the meantime I've made some soup, and there's new bread too. We'll eat in the kitchen, if you like, while she sleeps. She can have some when she wakes.'

He saw that Caitlin had barely touched her food. Flynn's own appetite faded similarly as he broodingly observed her from across the kitchen table.

The snow that blanketed the house and its surroundings muffled every sound, leaving an eerie silence in its wake—a silence that was akin to a still, frozen lake after all the birds had flown. But beneath the deceptive appearance of calm surely it was only a matter of time before something had to crack?

Her face was alabaster pale, and there were soft purplish and green smudges of fatigue beneath her vibrant blue eyes. She probably hadn't slept much since hearing of her father's death and coming home for the funeral. And she'd accused him of hurting her too, by making it hard for her to get close to him, and Flynn's conscience was pricked because he knew she was right.

Fighting hard against compassion, steeling himself against the treacherous attraction that flared just as fiercely as it had always done—despite his recent affirmation to Caitlin to the contrary—he suddenly pushed away from the table, his chair scraping loudly and discordantly against the stone-flagged floor, so that the silence was shattered as shockingly as breaking glass.

'If neither of us is going to eat then I may as well put on the kettle for some tea,' he ground out.

'We haven't talked about how often you'll want to see Sorcha after I go back to London.' Pushing aside the steaming bowl of aromatic soup she'd been unable to enjoy, Caitlin's voice was low. 'We ought to come to some arrangement since we're both stranded here for the night...don't you think?'

The sky-blue glance she settled on him was piercing in its pristine hue. For a moment Flynn was dazzled, and heat swirled into his belly with a deeply primeval force...the kind of heat that could enslave a man's desire for her for ever... Filling the kettle and placing it on the range, he fought through the debilitating fog of lust that had entrapped him, trying to centre himself.

'I've been giving that some thought,' he announced, turning back to face her.

'Well...would you like to share your views with me?'

'It's clearly nonsense to imagine we can make something work with you living in London and me here. Now that I've met Sorcha I know seeing her once or twice a month wouldn't be enough. Which is more than likely how it would go if we continue to live in separate countries. Our only real solution to the problem is for you and my daughter to move back here.'

'Back to Ireland?'

'Clearly the prospect doesn't appeal to you.'

Flynn could not curtail his profound dismay. But he was not about to let a second child slip out of his life so easily—even if the prospect of fatherhood daunted him more than ever because of what had happened between him and Isabel.

'It's not coming back to Ireland *per se* that doesn't appeal,' Caitlin answered softly, her brow furrowing. 'It's just that I've made a life for Sorcha and me in London, and she'd miss my aunt too much if we left. She's all the family she's known. I can't just uproot our whole lives without thinking about that.'

'Even if it's best for Sorcha?'

'How do you know it's best for her? How do *I*, for that matter? Parenthood is fraught with so many impossible choices.'

Flynn kept silent.

'I'll think it over… But I can't make any promises now,' she told him.

'Have you forgotten who I am, Caitlin? What I can give her? Her situation here would be much more secure… Would you deny her a better start in life than she's got now?'

'I wouldn't deny my child anything that was ultimately going to help her, but I have to consider my own position too, Flynn!'

'And what's that? You're a single mother, living in a big, careless city, trying to make ends meet by working in a bookstore!'

Even as Flynn spoke the words he felt a jolt of something painful tug at his heart. For the first time it crept into his consciousness just how tough that situation surely must be for Caitlin. It made him all the more determined to alleviate some of the

struggle—even if he was still disinclined to forgive
her for what she'd done.

'Since I've now acknowledged that Sorcha is
mine, it stands to reason that I should support her—
and *you* as her mother.'

'*Help* support her, don't you mean?' Pushing
her fingers agitatedly through her hair, Caitlin
stared at him with growing anxiety in her eyes.
'I'm willing to accept that our child should be a
shared responsibility...and I wouldn't deny Sorcha
your support...not if you're willing to give it. But
I need a measure of independence too. I'm used to
working...to taking care of things. And last time I
looked jobs were few and far between in this part
of the world. I can't just come back here and let you
take over everything, start making all the decisions
where the both of us are concerned!'

'I'm not taking over everything! And *I* am
Sorcha's family now, as well as you and your aunt!
Do you think I could stand back and watch her go,
knowing that if you both lived here she wouldn't
have to struggle at all? There'll be opportunities
here with me that won't be open to her is she stays
in your current situation in London. You talk about
impossible choices. Is it really so hard to make the
decision between penury and wealth?'

Taking a deep breath, Flynn moved restlessly
from one end of the room to the other.

'Moving into Oak Grove with me is your only

sensible choice. You certainly can't stay in your father's old place. Seeing it the other day, I was appalled by its unkempt and rundown condition! I certainly wouldn't want any child of *mine* living in such squalor!'

Caitlin shot to her feet. 'It's not unkempt! How dare you? My dad may have neglected the general upkeep of the cottage a bit—he was a one-man band, trying to work and take care of things on his own when I left, and there was very little money for luxuries—but there's no need to look down your nose at what was our home! We may have been poor but my parents were honest and hardworking! After I lost my mum it wasn't easy for my dad…but he did the best he could with the resources he had and I've nothing to be ashamed of. So don't you *dare* act so superior just because you've come from money and I haven't!'

Her breasts were heaving in her soft blue sweater, and her face was flushed with temper, and for a moment it was hard for Flynn to hang on to any desire to argue. Not when a quite *different* desire was storming through his veins.

'You sound just like your father. He had a real chip on his shoulder about wealth too! Stop being so damned defensive and see some sense, will you? Whatever way you look at it, who in their right mind could argue that Sorcha wouldn't be better off living here in comfort in Ireland than in a situation in London where you're struggling to put food on the table?'

'It's not as bad as all that! I don't earn a fortune, but I've made it work with my aunt's help for the past four years!'

'With your aunt's help?' His tone was disparaging. 'So you and Sorcha are living in *her* house, on her say-so? What kind of security is that for a child?'

'She's loved and cared for! That's the kind of security she has in abundance! Something that you and your own family clearly don't set a lot of store by!'

'And whose fault is it that I haven't been able to love my own daughter? I didn't even know of her existence until a couple of days ago! Answer me that while you're busy being so damn self-righteous!'

A stricken look came over Caitlin's face. 'I'm sorry,' she whispered brokenly.

As she started to turn away, Flynn was by her side in two long-legged strides, gripping her arms, his expression caught somewhere between intense frustration and despair.

'That word again!'

Would he ever forgive her? Staring up into that carved, long-boned, troubled face, Caitlin found it hard to see a way out of the fog of misery that had descended.

'You have to give me some time to think over what you've suggested. I—'

'Mummy!'

The rest of her words were cut off by the sound of her daughter's frightened cry.

His expression alarmed, Flynn had left the kitchen even before Caitlin. Reaching the living room, they found Sorcha sitting bolt upright on the couch, her hair a golden tangle from lying on the cushion, her pretty face damp with tears.

'Mummy's here, darling! What's the matter? Did you have a bad dream?'

Pulling her into her arms, Caitlin cradled the child against her, feeling the slight body tremble. Her own heart was beating much too fast.

'I dreamt that you went away and never came back! Just like my daddy did!'

Flynn's gaze locked with Caitlin's, something close to devastation reflected in his haunting jade eyes. For a moment Caitlin didn't think she breathed...

'I haven't gone anywhere, angel! I've been here all the time, with—' Her mouth went dry as sand. 'With your daddy.'

Lifting his hand, Flynn pushed away some of the hair from his daughter's tear-damp face. His lips were trying to curve into a smile, but seemed to be having some difficulty in completing the manoeuvre.

'Hey, beautiful. You know what? I'm not going anywhere soon without you. That's a promise.'

Stopping her quiet sniffling, Sorcha struggled to sit up in her mother's enfolding arms. Her gaze upon Flynn as he crouched down by her side was unwavering and direct.

'You mean you really will be my daddy—for ever?'

CHAPTER SIX

WHEN he stirred in the early hours, his duvet a crumpled mound over his body where he'd apparently wrestled with it during the night, Flynn knew that he'd hardly closed his eyes. All night long his racing thoughts had driven him near crazy, and his memory had played back time and time again the look on Sorcha's face and her sweet infant voice when she had asked him if he would always be her daddy.

An exceptionally perceptive child for her age, she had obviously thought about the fact that there had been no father figure in her life since she'd been born. Damn Caitlin! How could she have done that to him? Walked away like that when she knew she was carrying his baby? And yet allowing his affection for the little girl to deepen and grow would be no easy feat after the trauma of losing Danny. What if Caitlin decided one day that she didn't want him to be in Sorcha's life after all? What then? Dear God, he'd likely end up going mad if that happened! When Isabel had taken Danny away for a long time afterwards he had felt like a broken man.

Cursing the dread that loomed up inside him at the prospect of a similar scenario occurring, Flynn groaned out loud and dropped his head into his hands. It didn't help. It just seemed to stimulate more unwanted and troubling thoughts, and it was his thoughts that he was so desperately trying to get away from. Easing himself up into a sitting position, he rearranged the rumpled duvet and tugged it up to his shoulders. The temperature in the room was icy and his body shivered with cold. It was six in the morning, and as black as pitch outside, his head was pounding and his eyes felt as though someone had thrown a handful of sand in them. Usually he welcomed any opportunity for solitude… Right now he wanted anything *but*.

His fears were almost too much to bear by himself, and he decided he might as well get up as sit there plagued by demons. But, not wanting to disturb the two females sleeping downstairs, he hesitated. The knowledge that Caitlin was not far away had hardly assisted his aching, restless body during the night either. His libido was as entranced and taunted by her presence as it had always been—even though she had so badly let him down and he couldn't trust her.

Determined not to venture into even more unhelpful areas of his mind, Flynn strove to insert a little clarity into his thoughts. *First things first...* To help himself come to, and banish the effects of a night with no sleep, he badly needed some strong black coffee. Perhaps he would risk going down into the kitchen after all, to make some? After that, when Caitlin had risen and got dressed—he tried not to think of her wearing the white linen shirt he had lent her to sleep in—he would have an earnest conversation with her about his plans for their daughter's future welfare. For, in spite of his thoughts giving him no peace, what he wanted had suddenly become very clear to him...even though he couldn't fully acknowledge the reasons why.

'I've thought about what you suggested yesterday. About me and Sorcha moving back to Ireland and coming to live with you.'

Staring at Caitlin across the breakfast table as she spoke, Flynn knew his mercurial gaze was immediately alert.

'And?'

Outside, the relentless fall of snow had at last abated, and everything as far as the eye could see was thickly shrouded in an extra-generous coating of frosted white. Even Sorcha's snowman had doubled its girth.

'And...I've decided that we'll do it.'

The small but painful nugget of tension between

Flynn's shoulderblades eased. Suddenly he could breathe again without impediment. He'd thought he'd have a fight on his hands about the matter. He was stunned that she had conceded so easily in the end.

'What made you decide?' he asked, his voice a little gravelly because he hadn't slept.

She shrugged and put down the mug of tea she nursed. 'Everything you said last night made sense, I suppose. I think it's only fair that you should have a proper chance to get to know Sorcha, and she you…but only if you're certain that's what you really want?'

'I'm certain.'

Everything outside was still frozen, but inside Flynn's beleaguered heart something had thawed.

'So there's nothing to stop you both moving in with me today?'

'*Today?*'

'Why not? The sooner the better, as far as I'm concerned.'

'It can't be today, Flynn.'

Apprehension sounded in Caitlin's voice, and Flynn wondered briefly if she was already regretting her decision. But in the next instant he was thankfully reassured.

'I've still got my dad's things to sort out and get rid of, and the cottage to tidy before I give the keys back to the landlord. Plus, I—'

'Your father didn't *own* the cottage?'

'Of course he didn't!' Touching her fingers briefly to her lips, Caitlin sighed. 'My parents could never afford a mortgage. Unskilled work doesn't pay a lot, and my father worked the land all his life. They rented the cottage from Ted MacNamara. He said I could stay there as long as I wanted to after dad's funeral, but obviously he knew I had to go back to London at some point.'

If her father *had* owned the place then she and Sorcha might have had a bit of a nest egg for the future, Caitlin mused, but no such luck. Still, she was a pragmatist if nothing else, and there was no use crying over spilled milk. Having spent most of the night tossing and turning—mulling over and over the fact that Sorcha seemed to be forming a definite attachment to Flynn, and the idea of him being a permanent fixture in her life—she had concluded that the prospect of crucifying herself with even more guilt for depriving her daughter of a daddy and Flynn of his child was too much of a burden to be going on with. That was why she had decided in the end to comply with his suggestion about their moving back to Ireland.

'Then you've definitely made the right decision.' Flynn was on his feet in a trice. 'And, while we're on the subject, I've also thought about you going back to London. After Sorcha getting so upset last night, I've decided the only way you're going to go back and get your things and draw a line under your life there is if I go back with you. I'm not risking you either changing your mind or…more importantly…Sorcha believing that I've deserted her.'

Her heart tripping at the look of steel on his face, Caitlin absorbed his announcement with genuine shock. It took her aback that Flynn was sounding so possessive about the child he had only just met. It stunned her that he should care enough about Sorcha being upset that he would postpone his no doubt busy and demanding life to travel back to London with them and stay there until Caitlin had tied up the loose ends of her life there. Perhaps some of those hidden depths she'd long suspected him of harbouring were beginning to show…

'I'm not going to change my mind now that I've made my decision, and I'd never let Sorcha think you had deserted her! I'd reassure her that we'd be coming back to you. But, while we're on the subject, I have to tell you that the prospect of staying at Oak Grove doesn't exactly fill me with confidence. What will your family think of the arrangement? And, more to the point, what are they going to think about me turning up with your child?'

'Their opinion hardly signifies. The fact is, Oak Grove belongs to *me*—I live there and they don't! It's entirely up to me who I move in.'

Lifting his second mug of strong black coffee to his lips, Flynn took a long draught to finish the treacle-coloured brew and all but slammed the mug back down on the table. Wiping the back of his hand across his mouth, he threw Caitlin an impatient look, as if the subject was now definitely closed.

'I'll go and bring Sorcha in from the garden, and then we must get ready to leave. I don't want to risk another heavy fall of snow while we're travelling back down the mountain.'

Turning on his heel, he left Caitlin standing there.

She brought up the subject again on their journey home, and finally persuaded Flynn to agree to her and Sorcha going to stay at Oak Grove the following day instead. There were practical things to do to facilitate their move, and these would take time. Their suitcases had to be packed, and she needed to finish parcelling up the items her father had left which she was going to donate to the church for a future jumble sale. Plus, the cottage needed a thorough and final clean before she handed the keys back to the landlord.

But, most of all, Caitlin needed time to assimilate the events that were racing towards her with all the subtlety of a runaway juggernaut. She didn't doubt that Flynn was insisting on their move to his ancestral family home for Sorcha's sake and Sorcha's sake only. He was the type of man who would always meet his moral obligations, whether he welcomed them or not. She sighed. At least there was honour in him… But, although he might be dismissive of what his family would think of her and Sorcha turning up and moving in with him, Caitlin was nursing a real dread of being confronted by Estelle MacCormac again. The memory of her telling Flynn that Caitlin was more or less only using him for some kind of financial and material gain, and would probably try and trap him with a pregnancy, still had the power to revolt her.

The next day the temperature rose a couple of degrees, and the snow that had blanketed the countryside for days finally started to melt. The sound of ice dripping steadily off the cottage eaves provided a rhythmic backdrop to Caitlin and Sorcha's hearty breakfast of porridge, toast and marmalade.

There was a damp patch in a corner of the parlour ceiling that was leaking water. Discovering an old plastic bucket under the kitchen sink, Caitlin resignedly positioned it beneath the drip. It seemed to be a clear sign that the cottage definitely *wasn't* the place for her and Sorcha to see out the rest of their stay. Already it felt as if the damp and cold that the rundown dwelling reeked had taken up permanent residence inside her marrow.

Glancing at her watch, she saw that she had but half an hour before Flynn's promised arrival. In that time Caitlin had to clear the breakfast things, do a final check round, and leave the bags of jumble she'd sorted out on the back stoop, from where Father O'Brien from the church had promised to send someone to collect it.

Pausing for a moment between tasks, she had the strangest feeling that by agreeing to stay with Flynn she was casting her fate and Sorcha's into the great unknown, and the wild butterflies that seemed a given whenever she thought about him were suddenly back inside her stomach. At least in London—as difficult as life could be—she was resourceful and strong, and had faith in her ability to cope with most things. Becoming a single mother had definitely shaped her that way. But here in Ireland, around this enigmatic man who had turned her life upside down from the moment she'd set eyes on him, she felt anything *but*…

Her two frayed green suitcases looked starkly unprepossessing in the centre of Flynn's elegant sitting room floor. Like a shop-bought Christmas tree next to a sumptuous Norwegian Spruce. It was a dead certainty that they'd never been put down anywhere near as elegant before.

As Sorcha inquisitively skipped from room to room of their opulent new surroundings, Flynn indulgently having told her to explore wherever she wanted and make herself at home, Caitlin remained standing there in her duffle coat, jeans and sweatshirt, feeling as out of place as her unimpressive luggage.

'Aren't you going to take off your coat?' Shutting the door that led to the hall behind them, Flynn regarded her expectantly.

He wore casual clothing that was clearly not off the peg and was obviously expensive—and his unquestionably fit physique had all the bearing of a seasoned warrior from old Celtic tales of valour and honour. And with his black hair gleaming and newly washed, and his chiselled jaw freshly shaved, he was definitely possessed of all the beguiling attributes that could so easily ensnare a young girl's heart. Just as he had ensnared Caitlin's, at the tender age of just eighteen... Contemplating the prospect of living with him over the next few days, she couldn't deny she was feeling a little like an embattled fortress, under siege yet again.

'I'll take it off in a minute.' She smiled uncertainly. 'I'm still feeling the cold a bit, if I'm honest.'

Moving nearer to the warmth of the fire—presumably lit by his housekeeper—which beckoned welcomingly in the graceful surround of the fireplace, Caitlin stretched out her hands towards it.

'It's a wonder the pair of you didn't end up with pneumonia, staying in that draughty old cottage!'

Flynn remarked in exasperation. 'You should have come here yesterday, like I suggested.'

'I told you—I had things to do. As it is, there are bits and pieces of my dad's belongings that I just had to leave there. They wouldn't be of any use or interest to anyone…not even for a jumble sale.'

'If you want to keep some of them, I can find somewhere to store them for you, if you like?'

Her blue eyes mirrored her surprise. 'It's okay. It's not that important. I'm not sentimental about material things…just—'

'Just what?'

'It doesn't matter.'

To Flynn's examining gaze, Caitlin appeared extra pale and tired today. No doubt her recent bereavement was taking its toll, as well as the situation concerning him and Sorcha. He fought against feeling too much sympathy for her, yet something in him— some treacherously tender impulse—yearned to bring the light back to those pretty blue eyes.

Telling himself such a dangerous urge would likely be his downfall where she was concerned, Flynn yet again steeled his heart. Women couldn't be trusted. If he hadn't found that out by now, he really *was* in trouble. Celtic mythology was full of examples of the myriad ways the feminine sex practised to deceive. If he wanted to protect himself from future betrayal he should definitely not let his guard down for even a minute while he was around Caitlin.

'I'll take your cases into the spare bedroom. You and Sorcha should be quite comfortable in there.'

'Flynn?'

Her soft voice stopped him in his tracks.

'Do you know—can you guess how hard this is for me? Not just staying here in your house, but being here with you, knowing that you must hate me for what I did? How are we going to make things good for Sorcha if you won't even allow an opportunity for us to be friends?'

He shut his eyes for a moment, then opened them again. 'I'm not your enemy, Caitlin,' he said, with the suggestion of weariness in his voice, 'and I don't want you to feel unwelcome in my home. But right now we have to put Sorcha's needs and feelings before our own, to help her settle in. After that… Well…I've no powers to tell the future.'

Lifting the suitcases, he disappeared into an adjoining vestibule, then opened the door into what Caitlin knew from old was a sumptuous spare bedroom. In spite of her promise to herself to stay strong, emotion overtook her and her eyes welled up with tears. He seemed determined to maintain the distance between them by being aloof and detached, and he was not relenting towards her in any way. The hurt was immense.

By the time Flynn returned to the living room she'd scrubbed away all evidence of distress, taken off her coat, and silently vowed to make the best of a situation that was likely going to tax every sensibility she possessed. She owed that much to her daughter at least.

'At least the snow's started to melt.' Her glance towards the large Georgian windows was only brief, and she hardly registered the impressive view at all in her attempt at some light conversation to ease the tension.

'Hmm.' Clearly not predisposed to talk about the weather, Flynn narrowed his jade eyes. 'I've been meaning to tell you—'

There was a distinct rap on the door. In just a few long-legged strides he had crossed the large expanse of parquet floor to open it.

'Bridie,' he greeted the generously figured middle-aged woman who stood there, a patterned overall covering her clothes. 'Come in. I want you to meet Caitlin…and running round somewhere is Sorcha. I'm sure she'll find her way back to us in a minute or two. Caitlin, this is Oak Grove's housekeeper—Bridie Molloy.'

'Pleased to meet you, Bridie.'

Finding her hand clasped warmly in the older woman's, and faced with a pair of merry brown eyes that radiated both kindness and acceptance, Caitlin somehow sensed she'd found an ally. The previous housekeeper, Peg Donovan, had been *much* more formidable, and Caitlin had given her a wide berth whenever she'd seen her coming down one of the house's endless corridors towards her. Flynn had often used to tease her about her dread fear of the woman, then made it worse by telling her that as boys he and his brother had called her the 'ould witch'.

'I heard about your dad…I'm sorry for your trouble, my love. It's a hard thing to come home to, so it is.'

'Yes, it is.'

'Mummy! It's so big here it's like a palace! It's just like a king or a queen must live here!'

Bursting into the room, her golden hair a soft halo around her eager flushed face, Sorcha stopped shyly in her tracks when she set eyes on Bridie.

'Now, who can this beautiful young lady be?' The housekeeper smiled. 'If this is a palace, then I think she must be a princess…don't you Mr MacCormac?'

'Aye…she's definitely a princess.' Flynn's smile was like a sunburst as he turned his gaze upon his daughter. Watching him, Caitlin sensed her heart soar. 'Sorcha…come and say hello to Bridie.'

'Hello, Bridie.' She solemnly held out her small hand to the older woman.

Bridie crouched low, so that she was on the same level as the child, and her face was wreathed in delight as she gently shook it. 'Well, now. A princess, is it? I'm honoured, so I am!' Glancing up at Flynn and Caitlin she gave them a conspiratorial grin, 'What do you say I give Her Highness the royal tour of the house? And when we get to the kitchen there just might be some fairy cakes about ready to come out of the oven. Would you like a cake and a glass of lemonade, Your Highness?'

'Yes, please!'

Hopping from one foot to the other, Sorcha clearly had no qualms about going with the house-keeper for a while.

'Be a good girl, then, and mind your manners.' Dropping a kiss on top of the bright blonde head, Caitlin nevertheless reluctantly watched the child leave with the other woman, apprehensive at finding herself alone with Flynn when she wasn't at all prepared for such an event.

'She seems lovely,' she commented, as the housekeeper closed the door behind her.

'After the dour Peg Donovan, she's like a breath of fresh air!' Flynn agreed.

'What happened to Mrs Donovan? Did she—she didn't die?'

'Die?' His glance flared briefly with amusement. 'No…she didn't die. Would you believe she fell for a visiting gravedigger holidaying here for a while with his sister? She married him and went off to live in Dublin! We were all gob-smacked when it happened. It would have to be a strong fella with nerves of steel to take on our Mrs Donovan, that's for sure! But no doubt he was used to seeing a lot of frightening apparitions in his line of work!'

Caitlin couldn't help but laugh. Flynn's obvious enjoyment in telling her the unlikely story of his stern housekeeper's unexpected bid for romance contributed to the bubble of joy that suddenly burst inside her.

They both stopped smiling and laughing at the same time, and now the air crackled with something as different from humour as dark from light.

Feeling as though her skin had suddenly brushed up against electricity, Caitlin nervously tucked some stray blonde strands of hair behind her ear. 'You said you'd been meaning to tell me something before Bridie knocked at the door?'

Breaking out of the trance he seemed to have fallen into, looking at her, Flynn rubbed his hand round his jaw.

'I've been thinking about what you said about your independence…and you're right about jobs round here being thin on the ground. I wondered if you'd consider helping me out with some administrative stuff now and again? I'd pay you, and it might help alleviate some of your concern that I'm somehow taking control of your life. What do you think?'

Now it was Caitlin's turn to be gob-smacked. She definitely hadn't expected such an olive branch.

'Seriously?'

'I'm perfectly serious.' He allowed a rueful smile, and Caitlin's heart gave a little skip. 'You only have to take a look at the pile of unanswered correspondence on my desk to know that I'm definitely in need of some help!'

'When would you like me to start—and what about Sorcha?'

'Take a couple of days to settle in first, and I'll talk to Bridie. I'm sure she'll be only too happy to watch out for Sorcha while you work.'

'All right. Then I accept your offer. Thank you.'

CHAPTER SEVEN

IT WAS late in the evening and Flynn was in his study working. His concentration was hardly what it should have been, considering he had a book to deliver to his publisher by the end of the month, but right now ancient Celtic chieftains' plans for reinforcing their fortresses and their strategies to protect their *tuath*s against invaders from across the sea did not rivet his attention as emphatically as they usually did.

For one thing, he wasn't alone in the huge apartment, as he normally would have been. Every now and then during the day his attention would be diverted by the sound of his daughter's laughter, or her mother's calmly voiced reply. Sounds that even the thick oak doors that guarded the various rooms could not completely dim because Flynn was so intimately attuned to them. He had even found himself deliberately listening out for them. They'd been living with him for almost two whole days now, and already the pattern of his quiet, fairly ordered existence had been altered irrevocably.

At some point during each day Caitlin would take herself and Sorcha off on a longish ramble around the estate, and if Flynn hadn't already known she had a passionate penchant for fresh air whatever the weather—he would have been seriously impressed by her dedication to being in the great outdoors. That was one of the things he'd found so irresistible about her when they'd first met...her appreciation of the elements and her love and respect for nature, which he shared.

Both Caitlin and Sorcha spent a lot of time with Bridie while Flynn worked on his book, and he'd arranged with the housekeeper for their dinner to be brought up to his own private dining room in the evenings, so that Caitlin wouldn't feel things were uncomfortably formal. He'd seen the strain on her face, and he didn't want any tension she felt affecting her relationship with their daughter. Instead he wanted to help her realise that this was their home now.

After dinner he chose to spend time with Sorcha, playing or reading her a story before bedtime. He tried not to think too much about the hopes he'd had when Danny was born of doing the same with his son, but already Flynn had grown to anticipate the precious moments with his daughter with increasing pleasure. It was *after* Sorcha had gone to bed that was proving the most testing time for him. Even if he decided to go back to his study and continue working into the early hours of the morning, as he was doing now, he still had to deal with the fact that Caitlin would have settled herself in an armchair by the crackling fire, her head in a book, her feet bare and her soft blonde hair a golden and too touchable cloud around her head.

His body inconveniently tightened and he shifted in his chair. Why couldn't he trust himself to be alone in the same room with her? That wasn't difficult to answer. His body's lustful craving for her hadn't diminished any, despite the tension between them. He sighed and stared unseeingly at the screen on his desk. Whatever came about he was going to do everything in his power to get Caitlin to realise that she was better off here in Ireland with him. There was no way he was going to risk losing Sorcha like he'd lost Danny. The allure of her old life in London would surely soon diminish…and as he'd said to her, who would choose penury and struggle over wealth?

Flynn would just have to live with the fact that he himself would never be the main attraction, and it didn't matter that Caitlin still had misgivings about staying with him at Oak Grove—somehow she would have to learn to live with her reticence and weather the changes, just as Flynn had to.

Shutting down his computer, he stood up and

stretched with a yawn. Glancing down at his watch, he saw how late it was. As he walked across the room towards the door he told himself he was just going to have to somehow learn to stem the irrefutable urge to touch Caitlin whenever she was around. He hoped that she had yet again decided to have an early night. *Liar!* he silently mocked himself as his hand curved expectantly round the door handle. He was praying that she would still be sitting in the armchair, reading her book…

'Good book? It must be if you're still up reading at this hour.'

Tearing herself away from the compelling Celtic tales of heroic journeys, heartfelt challenges and lost loves she'd been reading, Caitlin stared up at Flynn's tall dark figure in his black sweater and jeans like someone in a trance.

Her father had often accused her of having one foot in this world and the other in a realm unseen, and he'd probably been right. As a child she had avidly scoured the surrounding woodland for sprites and fairies, and she had talked to imaginary friends whenever she was lonely or afraid. She'd also stared up at the sky and made castles, birds and animals out of the cotton-wool clouds that softly scudded by.

So many times she'd longed for something magical to happen, to take her far beyond the predictable pattern of her days. She'd feared even then that her future might hold a similar soul-destroying design as her parents, lives with nothing but struggle, and working hard, and no joy to lighten the load and look forward to. Caitlin had yearned for a world that promised enchantment and a love that would last for ever. When she had met Flynn her heart had beat so fast because she'd truly believed she'd found it.

Now, as he walked towards her, his aquamarine gaze reflecting spellbinding lights of blue-green fire as he rested it on her, she knew she couldn't hide her heartfelt need for him quickly enough. Laying down the book, she attempted to divert him.

'It's one of yours...I hope you don't mind? I helped myself from the bookshelf.'

'Let me see.'

To Caitlin's intense alarm, Flynn crouched down beside her and plucked the book from her lap. After examining the cover for a moment, he flicked idly through the pages. All the while she couldn't tear her eyes from his face, from the blue-black lights that glinted fiercely in his hair and his hard chiselled jaw, and neither could she ignore the warm, sensually musky scent that drifted up to her from his body.

'Which story are you reading? The tale about Deirdre and Naoise?' His mouth softened a little as he said this, but only someone who'd been on intimate terms with his moods and expressions would have detected such an infinitesimal change. 'So you like tales about wicked women who put spells on innocent young men and get them to elope with them?'

'Naoise was a warrior…a champion. Hardly an innocent.'

'Maybe. Clearly you still enjoy them? The old tales?'

'They're magical, and they have a purpose too. There's deep wisdom in the telling of them, and they can teach us so much about life. I've always loved them…you know that.'

She couldn't help but think of Flynn when she thought of the handsome warrior that the maiden Deirdre had indeed eloped with. He'd had hair as black as a raven's wing and had been heartbreakingly handsome, so the tale went…

Her voice had unwittingly lowered, and Flynn put the book aside. But instead of moving away, as Caitlin had expected, he stayed exactly where he was. The fire that danced with orange and blue flames in the fireplace next to them made the haunting lights in his eyes like the effect of sunlight on a still blue-green lake. Caitlin was caught in the spell of them, her whole body holding itself in abeyance. Almost in slow motion he slid his hand behind her neck and brought her head down to his.

The first touch of his lips was like cool satin

overlaid with velvet. Overwhelmed, relieved—
hungry to assuage an ache she hadn't even realised
she was nursing—Caitlin gasped her need into his
mouth. Behind her neck Flynn's warm hand grew
firmer, to hold her still so that he could drink from
the fountain of her lips as thirstily as he desired.

If she'd forgotten what the taste of heaven was
like, she remembered now. A wild tremor shivered
through her body at the pleasure he was igniting—
a profound, shuddering, soul-deep pleasure that
melted her as easily as the winter sun had melted
the icicles hanging from the cottage eaves the other
morning. Then he moved his hand from her nape
to follow the path of her spine, and soon after he
was urging her down onto the rug beside him,
touching her breasts through her shirt and dragging
her hips towards his so that she felt his growing
desire hard against her.

Their lips were magnets for one another,
clinging and tasting, stoking a fire that felt as if it
had been kindling all these years, just waiting to
burst into flame again. Drawing back with a ragged
breath, Caitlin glanced up into Flynn's passion-
darkened eyes with a question in her own dazed
blue.

'What?' he murmured, gravel-voiced, impatient to draw her back into another hungry and
sensual embrace.

'What are we doing, Flynn?'

'You mean you don't know?' He raised a dark brow with grim mockery. Feeling a cold shiver slither down her spine, Caitlin sensed her desire start to cool. This wasn't about *love*…she knew that. And, whilst the knowledge was apt to shatter her still unmended heart into a thousand tiny fragments yet again, she also knew it had very little to do with affection or regard either. None of those attributes had she sensed in Flynn's ardent demand. Nor would she, when all he seemed bent on was a kind of revenge for what he saw as Caitlin's deliberate rejection of what they'd once had. This was purely and simply about sex…about answering a primeval white heat that would scorch them both but leave Caitlin ultimately feeling like a used and empty well.

She would sacrifice much for her child, but she would not give her body to a man who neither loved nor respected her. No matter how powerfully she desired him. Extricating herself from his hold, she eased up onto her feet.

'I don't—I don't know what I was thinking. This can't happen between us. You know it can't. We need to implement some strict rules about this sort of thing while I'm here.'

'Rules, is it now?'

A sardonic smirk touched the lips that only a few moments ago had been devouring hers. He stood up beside her and his frustration was easy to sense. His hard, lean body radiated it.

'You wanted it as much as I did!'

His harsh accusation spared her nothing, and made Caitlin's face burn.

'Desire means nothing without love,' she commented sadly, hugging her arms over her chest.

'You stand there and talk about love when you walked out on me as if my regard meant less to you than some "blow-in" you'd only known for five minutes? Love!' He spat out the word, as though he scorned the very sound of it.

'You've become so bitter, Flynn. Did I do that?'

'What do *you* think?'

The look he gave her practically froze the blood in her veins, and Caitlin nervously touched her hair before turning her face away in a bid to hide the grief and despondency that welled up inside her.

'I know I said I left because of all the family opposition we had to us being together, and because the rows with my dad about us were getting me down...I didn't lie.' Choosing her words carefully, she swallowed hard before continuing. 'But there was so much more to it than that, Flynn.'

'Go on.'

His stern visage hardly invited her confidence, but then Caitlin was used to that. Somewhere along the line she had to find a way through her reticence and doubt and risk telling him the truth. How could there be any chance of an improvement in their relations if she didn't?

Sighing, she made herself continue. 'Would I have left a man I trusted with all my being as well as loved? My father hardened his heart and didn't let me anywhere near after my mother died. He probably did it unconsciously, to protect himself, but it still hurt. Then I met you—and you did the same! You were kind to me, yes, and you wanted to be with me. You made that clear…with your body, with your eyes. But you rarely gave me any insight into the real man. There was a distance between us even then, Flynn, and I defy you to deny it! How could I tell you what was in my heart—let alone that I was pregnant with your child—when you never revealed anything to me about what might be in your own? I still don't know what ails you…why you hold back so. Maybe you can tell me something…*anything*…that would give me a clue?'

Something flared deep in his eyes, but his lips remained sealed. Caitlin knew instinctively that sometimes secrets were not revealed in actual words, yet silence could touch upon so much. She sensed the power of silence now, and made herself wait. And if she added a prayer or two to help things along, then only she was privy to that.

'This isn't the first time I've believed myself to be a father.'

Now Caitlin was stricken silent, but the thud of her heartbeat sounded like cannonfire in her ears.

Flynn's hand tunnelled restlessly through his thick dark hair, but his gaze remained steady as he continued to focus it on her.

'I told you I was married before, and that I ended up divorcing the woman in question? Well…she had a baby. A little boy named Danny. For six months I believed him to be mine…that I was his father. Then she told me she'd been having an affair, and the child was this other man's. She'd had a paternity test done to prove it. Her lover had insisted on it, and because she was in love with him and not me she agreed. For six months she let me think I was the boy's father—until finally her lover gave her an ultimatum and told her to choose between the two of us. Well, she chose her lover. And, taking Danny with her, she moved out and went to live with him. That's it. End of story.'

Turning away, Flynn laid his hand on the marble mantelpiece over the fire.

Remaining where she stood—partly out of shock and partly because she sensed he needed some space right now—Caitlin's deeply affected gaze never left his haunting, absorbed profile.

'But that's *not* the end of the story…is it, Flynn?' she questioned him softly. 'You're still hurting over what happened. You miss your son. Oh, God! If only you'd told me this when we were first together!'

'So you'd have stayed with me out of sympathy?' His glance was brutal. 'I don't think so!'

'It's not about sympathy, Flynn! Though I wouldn't be human if I didn't feel for you in such a cruel situation. It's about allowing *intimacy*...trust. It's about knowing that your secrets are safe with me and mine with you.'

'That's as maybe. But what happened isn't something a person gets over in five minutes! And then to have *you* walk away...' He clenched his jaw, as if contemplating so much perceived betrayal was too much to bear, then turned and crossed the room to the door. 'I'll leave you to enjoy your book in peace. Goodnight, Caitlin. I'll see you in the morning.'

She knew there was no point in going after him. Not now, when all he really wanted was to be alone and tend to his wounds in private. But what he'd told her was a revelation that gave her more than just a small clue to his aloof, detached persona, and somewhere deep inside her Caitlin knew it was a breakthrough.

Almost too restless to contemplate sleep, she chose to stay up long into the night reading instead—but her thoughts were not on the pages of print in front of her. They were on Flynn, and the little boy that his ex-wife had cruelly taken away, whom he had clearly loved deeply...

After that, was there room in his broken heart for her and his daughter?

CHAPTER EIGHT

'There's something I've been thinking about,' Flynn announced the next morning, as they breakfasted together in his private dining room.

'Can I get down now, Mummy?' Sorcha interrupted, eager to get back to the toys that Bridie had brought yesterday, which had once belonged to her own now grown-up daughter.

Leaning forward to wipe some strawberry jam off the child's rosebud mouth with a linen napkin, Caitlin nodded. 'Go on, then. But you'd better get Bridie to take you to the bathroom and brush those teeth before you do anything else! I'll be checking to see if you've done them, mind!'

'All right.'

The soft green eyes demonstrated immediate reluctance for carrying out this mundane but necessary task, and Flynn couldn't help grinning. 'You'd better do as your mother says,' he advised, ruffling his daughter's bright hair. 'You don't want to end up like that "toothless old hag" in the fairy story I read you last night!'

Sliding off her chair, Sorcha placed her hands indignantly on her hips and affected a look of great mortal offence. 'I'm *not* going to be an old hag! I'm a princess, and a princess stays young and beautiful for ever! Silly Daddy!' And off she flounced, completely unaware that she'd left Flynn sitting there with astonishment written all over his face.

'I swear she's a sixty-three-year-old in the body of a child!'

Shaking her head in amusement, Caitlin smiled. Having naturally noted her daughter's poignant reference to Flynn as 'Daddy', and thinking about the secret from his past that he had so reluctantly revealed last night, she hoped her smile hid the sudden wave of emotion that deluged her.

'You said there's something you've been thinking about?' Taking a careful sip of her hot cup of tea, she settled her wide blue eyes expectantly on Flynn.

But he was still busy absorbing the incredible fact that his child had just casually addressed him for the first time ever as her daddy. He felt as if his heart had just burst wide open.

'What was I saying?' He scraped his hand distractedly through his midnight hair, thinking hard. 'Ah, yes... Two things occurred to me after we'd spoken last night.' His eyes sought hers.

For a long moment their gazes clung, surprised, enthralled, as if they couldn't bear to look away from each other, then Caitlin blushed deeply, and carefully returned her cup to its matching porcelain saucer.

Flynn had always loved that 'shy' aspect to her personality, and he discovered that that hadn't changed.

She was looking exceptionally pretty this morning—a factor that seemed to provoke a deep carnal heat in him that uninhibitedly travelled to his groin as he gazed at her. Reflecting on the events of last night, he wryly recalled that they'd done a bit more than speak. He was riveted by the way the soft pink sweater she wore clung to the sweet perfection of her lovely breasts, unknowingly inviting his ardent examination and increasing his rather inconvenient desire. Endowed with the kind of lovely, unforgettable face that any man would thrill to find on the pillow next to him in the morning on waking, Caitlin also had the body of a siren. The combination was intoxicating. And motherhood had clearly enhanced those stunning attributes.

Although she had sworn to him that there had been no intimate relationships for her during the past four years, Flynn wondered if she'd ever got lonely for the feel of someone's arms around her. She wouldn't be human if she hadn't—but it damn near killed him to think of her with anyone else but him. After his unexpected confession last night, he had to own to feeling particularly vulnerable where she was concerned.

'First of all we need to talk about when you're planning on going back to London.'

'We're due to leave this Saturday…I told you. Are you still intending to come with us?'

'Of course. But we can't return this Saturday— that's what I wanted to talk to you about. I need you to postpone the trip for another couple of weeks at least.'

'Another couple of weeks? Why?'

'Because my workload is such that I just can't leave it.'

'Then why can't Sorcha and I travel back on our own and you can join us?'

'No.'

'What do you mean, *no*?'

Flynn immediately detected that his seemingly inflexible attitude had upset her. But he had his reasons for not wanting her to leave without him, and in his opinion they were sound ones.

'You're not taking my daughter anywhere without me.'

'Be reasonable, Flynn! We *have* to go home on Saturday! My plane tickets aren't transferable for one, and secondly I need to let them know at work what I'm doing. I might have to work a week or two's notice before they'll let me leave.'

'You don't need anyone's permission to quit your job, and you won't be working *any* notice.' His tone disapproving, Flynn coolly conveyed his intransigence on this point. 'There's no need. You're simply going to tell them you're resigning for personal family reasons, and that your resignation has to take effect straight away. In fact, the more I think of it, you could probably deal with the whole thing on the telephone and follow it up with a letter.'

'And what about my aunt?'

'What about her?'

'She's expecting us home! What am I going to tell her?'

'Tell her that *I'm* going to take care of you and Sorcha now.'

'I don't need taking care of! I'm not a child.'

Caitlin's darkly golden brows had creased in protest. Determinedly Flynn tried to deflect her unhappiness.

'Think about it… You could probably do with a break after what's happened with your father. Surely your aunt understands that? What's the urgent need to go back to London? You're basically resigning from your job and packing a few things for you and Sorcha. Apart from that…you're free.'

'Free?' Her blue eyes visibly darkened. 'That's a strange way to put it! As if there's no emotional attachment to the place I've lived for the past four and a half years at all! I'm not saying I'll exactly miss London, but I will miss my aunt. She's my closest friend, as well as my relative. We've been through a lot together.'

Her comment instigated a train of thought that instantly perturbed him. Reflecting on the momentous event of her having had a child alone, without him as the father to support her emotionally as well as materially, Flynn all but winced. He should have been there with Caitlin to help her when she had Sorcha. If he could have been—he would have been.

'We were friends too, once upon a time,' he replied thoughtfully, his huskily voiced words making her glance up at him with surprise. 'Remember, Caitlin?'

He barely heard her reply, it was so quiet. 'I remember.'

'So that's settled, then? The London trip is postponed until I finish my work?'

'If there isn't any other way round it, I suppose it is. Look…if you're feeling overwhelmed you should let me help you, like you suggested. We could start today, if you like?'

Again she had surprised him. He'd thought he'd have a royal battle on his hands about delaying her trip back to London, but instead it seemed she'd chosen to acquiesce with his wishes rather than argue. Was that because of what he had revealed last night? Flynn abhorred the idea that Caitlin was, after all, feeling sorry for him.

'Why not?' he agreed, shrugging. 'I'll talk to Bridie about looking after Sorcha for a while. There's something else too…'

Automatically starting to clear away the breakfast things, Caitlin paused.

'I've been thinking about our living arrangements.' Folding his arms across his chest, he exhaled a resigned-sounding sigh. 'It came to me that you might be happier and more comfortable if you and Sorcha occupied the apartment in the east wing rather than stay here with me. You would have your own private space and yet still be under my roof. What do you think?'

She noted he'd asked what she *thought*, not how she *felt*. Somewhere hurt and dismay surfaced, because she wondered if he wasn't subtly trying to keep her at a distance. Determinedly, she pushed away her doubt.

'I think it sounds like a good idea,' she heard herself say, though she was not at all convinced.

'The other thing I've been meaning to ask is, can you drive?' Flynn continued. 'I know you hadn't had any lessons when we were first together…'

'I still haven't.' Pursing her lips for a moment, Caitlin was genuinely rueful. 'I wish I could drive, but there was no need to learn living in London. I simply used public transport. I know it's a very different kettle of fish getting around here.'

'Then I'm going to arrange lessons for you as

soon as possible. I'll get you your own car, and you can have all the freedom you want. Perhaps living with me might not be so difficult for you then? How does that sound?'

It sounded as if he was being both generous and thoughtful, despite his reference to living with him being difficult, and Caitlin knew it would be churlish to complain. Having her own apartment in the house and her own space was probably wise at this point in time, when things between them were still under somewhat of a strain. Even though there had been that breakthrough of his story about the boy he'd believed to be his son—a first in terms of personal confessions from the heart...

Going back to the issue of their living arrangements, it crossed her mind that perhaps she and Sorcha disturbed Flynn during the day when he was working. Even though his apartment was huge by anybody's standards. Yet she couldn't help returning to the thought that he'd leapt at any opportunity to install a little more distance between them. The barriers were still there, and he wasn't going to relinquish them easily. He was prepared to give Sorcha all the time in the world, but when it came to his ex-lover he still had no intention of letting his guard down.

'It's a kind offer on both counts, and I don't think I'll refuse. Thank you.'

Before Flynn could say anything else, she turned away to go in search of their daughter.

* * *

The spare apartment in the east wing was delightful. With its varnished wooden floors, high ceilings and light and airy aspect, there was enough space contained within it to house one large family or two smaller ones. Either way, Caitlin was unused to inhabiting the realms of such unmitigated luxury.

Once she'd unpacked her own and Sorcha's suitcase, hung their meagre selection of clothing in the cavernous wardrobes and then deposited their equally minimal toiletries in the vast luxurious bathroom, she found herself longing for some of her personal things from home to arrange around the place. She didn't have much, but she would have liked her photographs, her books and her CD collection at least. Never mind. At least the apartment was fully furnished with everything even the most discerning occupant might need or desire.

Suddenly restless, Caitlin walked over to the huge Georgian sash window in her bedroom, which overlooked the parkland where Flynn had taken an excited Sorcha to look at the horses. There was a hollow feeling in her stomach now, that seemed to have replaced her previous optimism that at last he might be more prepared to talk about his past and open up a little.

Perhaps she should have resisted his offer of living in a separate apartment from his? What if her acceptance had merely confirmed to him that she wanted to have as little to do with him as possible other than their dealings concerning Sorcha? That would be no good to them at all! It was clear that he was still grieving for the little boy he'd lost, and Caitlin turning up after all these years with Sorcha had surely dredged up aspects of his past that were clearly still blisteringly raw in their intensity. How could she get him to see that she wanted to *help* him heal by being with him…not make things worse?

But at least father and daughter seemed happy together. She should be relieved that Flynn hadn't rejected Sorcha altogether after what had happened to him before. Again she sensed the heavy cloak of guilt deaden her shoulders. Perhaps she didn't *deserve* happiness? What if her impetuous and frightened actions of four and a half years ago had robbed her of the possibility of being happy for ever?

The thought wasn't at all helpful—bruising her soul as it did—and, feeling impatience at indulging in such destroying self-pity, she elected to ring her aunt. Apart from seeking the comfort of someone who really cared about her, she needed to explain why she and Sorcha wouldn't be returning to London on Saturday after all. After that, she would get on with the task of resigning from her job.

There was a knock at the door. Having fallen into an exhausted doze on the sumptuous living room couch whilst reading her book, Caitlin guiltily jolted upright and hastily tried to fix her tousled hair as she hurried out into the vestibule.

'Flynn!'

'I just came to see if you were settling in okay. Bridie offered to take Sorcha into town to do some shopping. I let her go. Was that all right?'

'Yes, but—'

'Can I come in?' His expression inscrutable, he swept past her without waiting for a reply.

Caitlin stared after him, slightly muzzy-headed after being woken so abruptly. 'What's up? You look as if you've got something on your mind,' she commented, wondering what this visit was really about.

'Since you ask…there *is* something.'

Heading into the living room, with its air of calm and its gracious antique furniture and elegant rugs, Flynn waited for Caitlin to join him.

Her heartbeat slowed inside her chest as she saw the definite strain between his brows—as though the tension inside him was rendering any equilibrium or even a pretence at it impossible.

'I want you to tell me about Sorcha's birth,' he said, his jade eyes flaring with so many shades of feeling that Caitlin was momentarily struck dumb.

Of all the reasons for his unexpected visit, she hadn't expected this.

'What?'

'I need to know. I've been with her for the past couple of hours and I've been wondering…'

'Why don't you sit down and be comfortable? I'll willingly tell you anything you want to know.'

They sat on opposite sides of the couch she'd been dozing on, and Caitlin felt like a novice climber at the foot of her first significant mountain. Did she have the necessary courage to negotiate this particular daunting ascent?

'Where do you want me to start?' she asked.

'What was your pregnancy like?'

He sat with his elbows resting on taut long-boned thighs beneath dark denim jeans. A lock of sable hair slipped forward onto Flynn's brow, and Caitlin longed to sweep it tenderly back for him. But taking a deep breath, she started to recall what carrying her baby for nine months had been like.

'The first three months were the hardest, I think. I was awfully sick, and couldn't keep anything down. But after that…I just felt this incredible sense of well-being and rightness somehow. As if—as if Mother Nature herself was minding me in some way.'

She felt heat surge into her face, suddenly self-conscious, but Flynn was looking at her as though every word she uttered was somehow vital and im-portant. It spurred her on.

'The last six weeks were a bit of a challenge… moving around, I mean. I was used to nipping about like a two-year-old, and I felt slow and ponderous. I got very tired too. But Aunt Marie was wonderful, and encouraged me to rest whenever things got too much.'

'And what about the birth? What happened on that day?'

'I woke up at one in the morning with pains. I knew it was the real thing because I was about a week overdue. My aunt called an ambulance, and they came and took me into hospital. I was in labour for a night and a day.' She grimaced. 'There was a complication, and at one time the baby got a bit distressed inside the womb. They talked about giving me a Caesarean, but I so wanted to have my baby naturally! Somehow I knew it would be all right—blind faith, you might call it—and in the end it was. She had a fine pair of lungs on her right from the first moment she drew breath, I can tell you! I should have known from then on she'd come into the world with plenty to say for herself!'

Flynn sensed the tension inside him lock tight as he thought about Caitlin being in labour for so long. A night and a day, she'd said. When she'd first returned to Ireland and he had seen her, he had wanted retribution for what she'd done to him. Now, hearing about his daughter's birth, it made something that had previously been an abstract idea entirely personal—and very close to home. Now he found he couldn't even tolerate the thought of either Caitlin or Sorcha being in distress.

'And then, when you took her home...what was her sleeping like? Danny used to—' He abruptly cut off the thought that had crept up on him unawares, and the jolt it caused in the pit of his stomach was sickening.

'Danny used to what, Flynn?' Caitlin urged, gently leaning towards him, her blue eyes concerned. 'Was he a poor sleeper? Did you have to get up to him during the night?'

Slowly he let out the breath he was holding, that was near cutting him in two. His fingers found the wayward hair that flopped onto his brow and pushed it back to no avail. 'Several times sometimes. Isabel complained about being disturbed, so I saw to him. I never minded. It was an opportunity for the two of us to spend time alone together in the still of the night, with no one else around.' Hardly believing he was telling her all this, Flynn ruefully moved his head and swallowed hard over the intolerable ache in his throat.

'He must have meant so much to you.'

'Let's just concentrate on Sorcha, shall we? Tell me some more about her as a baby.'

He knew that she would have encouraged him to talk some more about the other child who had been in his life, but Flynn already felt he'd said too much about that. It was their daughter, the little girl who was quickly making dangerous inroads into his heart right now, that he needed to discuss.

Leaning back against the luxurious upholstery, Caitlin let a smile steal onto her lips like the sun peeping from behind a cloud. 'She was just adorable! She was surprisingly contented, in spite of everything, and she could sleep for England *and* Ireland, so thankfully there were no problems there! I'd never have entertained the thought of going back to work when she was eighteen months old if she'd had trouble sleeping. I don't think I could have coped with the lack of my own sleep and taking care of everything else.'

'But you *did* cope. And from what I can tell looking at Sorcha you did a grand job, Caitlin. Motherhood clearly comes naturally to you.'

'I don't know about that! I'm quite capable of making a hash of things sometimes. I'm not perfect, but I do my best. And I love her very much.'

'I can see that too.'

'Was there anything else you wanted to know?'

His answering smile seemed to come naturally...with hardly any reticence at all. 'I think that's fine for now...'

CHAPTER NINE

FOR a while Caitlin simply basked in the feeling of calm that swept over her after Flynn had spoken. It was a rare thing since she'd been back, and she wanted to savour it. His smile too had caught her unawares. Unguarded, like honey to a bee, it had made everything inside her feel as if it was indeed drowning in sweet enticing nectar.

But, finding him in this more conciliatory mood, she wanted some answers of her own. Replies to more personal enquiries that he might not have contemplated giving even just a day ago…

'Your ex-wife…Isabel…?'

Gazing directly up into a hypnotic glance that led her thoughts down a very provocative road indeed, Caitlin struggled to concentrate.

'What about her?' he asked.

'You never told me much when we were together…except—except that things didn't work out between you.'

'Nobody likes talking about being made a fool of by someone. Though the blame doesn't all lie with Isabel. I was the prize fool who kidded myself that I could somehow transform a travesty of a relationship into a real marriage…even though I quickly realised I'd mistaken physical attraction and lust for something more meaningful.'

'Why did you marry her, then?'

The question was out before she had fully realised her intention to verbalise it. When someone had been hurt, or carried a deep emotional wound, it wasn't necessarily the right thing to try and force a revelation, in Caitlin's opinion. One had to tread carefully. But, nonetheless, Flynn didn't hesitate in answering.

'A temporary lack of judgement capitalised on by family pressure.' He shrugged. 'They were all for it, and convinced me that everything would work out given time. She came from the right social strata, she was pretty, educated, and both sets of parents approved.'

'And the affair she had? That started *after* you got married?'

'Before, as a matter of fact.'

'And you had no idea that she was seeing someone else?'

He shifted in his seat and glanced momentarily away. 'I was glad she chose not to spend a lot of time at home. She had a tight-knit circle of friends, and she was always doing something with them…travelling, shopping, indulging herself on a regular basis. Until she told me she was pregnant I was more than happy for her to go her own way.'

'But you welcomed the news that you were going to be a father?'

There was a flash of the intense light in his eyes that Caitlin had seen reflected before, when he'd spoken about the little boy he'd lost, and her heart turned over.

'I did.'

'Oh, Flynn… It must have been terrible for you when you found out that—'

'Danny wasn't mine? *Terrible* is perhaps too mild a word. Anyway, I'm weary of talking about it. Do you mind?'

'So you never—you never see him?' Caitlin ventured one last question to complete the puzzle.

'Isabel and her lover moved to Italy after she left me. Apparently he had family there who offered him a home and a job. We both agreed that it was probably best I didn't keep in contact… She wanted Danny to have the chance to get close to his real father.'

'What a dreadful situation! You must have— It must have broken your heart into a million pieces!'

He neither moved nor spoke. Everything about that indomitable visage of his denoted great strength of mind, uncommon passion and purpose, but Caitlin was beginning to see that she had misjudged Flynn. She'd worried that he was incapable of great love towards anyone, but now she knew that the reverse was true. Underlying the words that had come so reluctantly and with such obvious difficulty when talking about the loss of the child who had clearly meant the world to him were emotions that ran fathoms deep.

He would never forget the little boy he had loved…not until his dying day. He'd carried the wound around with him for years, and the scarring must be indelible. Caitlin could hardly breathe for the hurt she felt on his behalf.

'You were Danny's father for a while, Flynn!' Leaning towards him, she reached out her hand and tenderly, so *carefully*, touched the side of his jaw. With the pad of her thumb she stroked across the shadowed stubbled surface. 'A part of that little boy's spirit will always know that—no matter where he is. Some part of him will know that there was this incredible man who loved him so much, and that can only enhance his own ability to love deeply when he grows to a man. That's your legacy to Danny. Love never dies, Flynn. It's a power…a force for good in the world like nothing else!'

'Sweet heaven!' Capturing her hand, Flynn turned it palm up and pressed his lips against the centre. His mouth was warm, intoxicating, a poem of tenderness and passion, and Caitlin sensed her need for him break all its bounds and make her very insides ache.

'No one but you could say such a thing…could even understand,' he told her, keeping hold of her hand and avidly examining her face.

'I meant it, Flynn. I so want to—'

'What?'

'I so want to show you—to tell you—'

Closing the gap between them even more, Flynn momentarily touched her lips with his fingers, then beguilingly brushed back a strand of her hair. 'Do you think I'd try and stop you?'

The room fell quiet, and a sensual undercurrent filled the air between them with an exquisite expectancy that was as taut as a harpstring.

'Do you not know that I'd die a thousand deaths if I couldn't touch you right now the way I yearn to touch you, Caitlin?'

Her blue eyes grew very wide…as though a sublime ocean of feeling resided in each.

The ancient Celts believed that in the act of gazing deeply into a lover's eyes, making love with them, your spirit inhabited theirs for a little while, and vice versa. It was a momentous thing. It reinforced an ancient and sacred circle of belonging that was there when your twin souls first recognised each other.

Staring into Caitlin's bewitching gaze now, Flynn remembered the quiet, yet explosive excitement that had erupted inside him that very first occasion when their glances had met. Whole futures spun and wove far-reaching webs on such moments. He'd known then that his own path would irrevocably be tangled up with hers.

Moving her into this vacant apartment, his desire had been to give her some space, so that she could grieve for her father in peace and by degrees come to see that living with Flynn at Oak Grove would have benefits—material ones, at least—that she might come to welcome as time went by. But the truth of it was he was having the devil's own job trying to resist her, and no distance was great enough to keep his desire for her totally under lock and key. Not when his whole body was consumed by the frustrating need to touch her on a daily basis.

'I feel the same.'

'Good.' His lips formed a smile that would stop the tides. 'Then let me take you to bed.'

Finding herself in that neat and orderly bedroom, where not so much as a loose thread on the dulled gold counterpane disrupted its perfect symmetry, Caitlin knew her wild emotions were the exact opposite. Now, with her limbs entwined with Flynn's, she knew she was exactly where she yearned to be. Where she was meant to be.

It was a joy unparallelled to have the freedom to slide her hands down that strong, lean back with its taut, well-developed muscles and silky skin, to feel that amazing well-defined mouth of his tasting her lips as though he was a man near desperate for air. And when that same voracious mouth turned its attention to her tingling, aching breasts, her passion-filled moans permeated the surrounding silence like something wild, suddenly released after long imprisonment.

How had she survived without this utterly necessary intimacy with this man for over four long years? Apart from Sorcha's presence to lighten them, the days had indeed been like prison walls—because her spirit had been here with him all this time…

'I feel like we're doing this for the very first time,' she admitted softly, her voice a broken whisper as she at last allowed herself the freedom to push back that rogue lock of coal-black hair from his lightly grooved forehead. 'I've missed you so, Flynn. I've longed for your touch.'

His mercurial glance blazed down at her.

'And do you know how long I've needed *your* touch?' he responded, his rich voice threaded with unconstrained passion.

'I never meant to hurt you.'

For a long, unsettling moment she sensed him grow still, and his gaze seemed to excavate deep inside Caitlin's soul. Her chest grew tight with trepidation. Fearing he might leave her, she started to withdraw her hand from where it lay across his tightly bunched bicep, her heart almost torn in two with despair at the idea that he'd changed his mind about making love to her. But then he emitted a harsh-voiced groan and kissed her hard—so hard that his teeth and lips connected bruisingly with hers.

'I need this. I need this like I will die if I don't have you! But I need to protect you too,' he told her, when he could finally bear to tear his lips from hers.

'It's all right, Flynn…I'm on the pill,' Caitlin answered quickly.

Anxious that he shouldn't think that it was because she'd been sleeping with anyone else, she started to explain that she took the oral contraceptive purely to ease her period cramps, but to her relief there was no doubt in his eyes, and with the sound of her own heartbeat drowning out further thought Caitlin sensed Flynn's hands slide firmly beneath her bottom, urging her hips towards him.

There was no gentling her for his possession. His uncontained hunger reached out to her and filled the wild, empty spaces in her own longing, so that when he took her with one long, penetrating deep thrust everything inside her softened willingly in answer. It had always been like this. The first heated touches when they'd been together had always elicited this raw, elemental explosion of need— and then, when that had been assuaged, would come the tender, quieter, yet equally fulfilling counterpoint of their loving.

The profound, soul-searching glare from Flynn's disturbing black-fringed jade eyes possessed Caitlin with as much hunger and need as his body did, and she couldn't hold back the ocean-tide of feeling that seemed to gather strength inside her until there was nowhere else for it to go. Instead it got caught up in a passionate eddy that made her release a cry of wonder and indescribable pleasure as it reached its zenith.

Her moans of satisfaction swiftly turned to tears of joy touching on regret. Why had she let him go when she should have held on to what she'd had with her life if need be? Why hadn't she been stronger and braver and somehow *made* him open up to her?

'Hush, now…hush…It's all right.'

Kissing her tears away, Flynn drove hard into her body and finally fell against her, his breathing harsh and his forehead lightly sheened with sweat. As the erotic scents from their skin mingled and the fragile winter light of the day started to edge its way towards afternoon Caitlin wrapped her arms around her lover and willed her tears of regret away. Instead of dwelling on the past, she would hold these precious moments to her like an unexpected matchless gift. And nobody could take that away from her.

Moving to her side, Flynn urged her against him, fitting her body into his as though she was the missing part of him he'd long been searching for.

Thinking back over their conversation earlier, when she had asked him about his ex-wife and his son, he knew a great longing to have trusted Caitlin more when they'd first met—to have shared the truth with her about what he'd been through. Maybe if he had she wouldn't have left as she had, and he wouldn't have spent all this time resenting her as well as blaming her father for her leaving. He was beginning to see that he had played a not 'insignificant' part in driving her away. He had been too quick to blame others, instead of looking at himself, and now Flynn saw that he'd allowed his ex-wife's cruel actions to make him bitter, closed-off, suspicious of anyone wanting to get close to him.

No wonder Caitlin had felt she couldn't trust him with the news that she was pregnant!

Storing away the information until he could properly consider it, Flynn tenderly stroked Caitlin's hair, then gently kissed the top of her silky head. 'Why don't you try and get some sleep?' he suggested. 'I'll get up and see to Sorcha when she returns.'

'I promised to help you with your work, remember?' she said, stifling a yawn.

'Work can wait.'

'Are you sure?'

'Absolutely.'

'Then in that case I might just take a nap—if you

promise me you'll stay a while?' As she murmured her reply, her eyelids clearly were struggling to stay open, and her warm breath feathered softly over Flynn's bare chest.

A few moments later he heard her sigh and knew she was sound asleep. Staring up at the high vaulted ceiling, he exhaled—perhaps the longest, most relaxed breath he'd experienced in ages. If it hadn't been for the fact that it was his daughter whose return he was awaiting nothing barring an act of God could have induced him to move from that bed. His spirit soared at having this beguiling woman back in his arms again. Being inside her, feeling her scalding velvet heat enfold him, as well as the erotic sensation of her long legs clasping his waist in passionate surrender, had been the culmination of a long-held dream. He'd missed her more than he could ever say.

And as Caitlin's hand splayed out against his back in sleep, the brush of her satin skin once again instigating his passionate arousal, Flynn battled hard to contain his longing for her. Sliding his hand down over the smooth, undulating contour of her hip, he found himself willing her to wake in time for him to have her again at least *once* more, before he absolutely had to get up and go and collect Sorcha from Bridie's care…

Later that afternoon, having left Flynn in his office taking a phone call, Caitlin followed her daughter down the grand curving staircase, watching closely to make sure she didn't fall and hurt herself as she skipped happily ahead. They were heading for the huge country-style kitchen, where Bridie had promised to spend some time making iced buns with Sorcha so that Caitlin could help Flynn with his work.

Outside, the dull weather had been lifted by a welcome display of fierce sunshine, and nearly all of the snow that had covered the countryside for days was gone, leaving a shimmering verdant landscape in its wake. Caitlin was sensing a sea change of hope arise inside her since making love with Flynn, and her mood was buoyant. As they reached the bottom step a figure appeared through the opened front door at the end of the hallway—a familiar figure that took her aback.

It was Estelle MacCormac—Flynn's mother. Despite the shock that ebbed through her like icy ocean waves, Caitlin determinedly tried to cling onto her upbeat mood. Why hadn't Flynn mentioned she was coming today? She would at least have been better prepared for the confrontation.

The older woman was the epitome of elegance, dressed in a black coat over an emerald-green tailored suit and cream blouse, a rope of antique pearls at her neck. Immediately conscious of her own less elegant attire, of serviceable black sweater and jeans, Caitlin sensed her heartbeat drum hard.

Estelle's critical gaze seemed to freeze on mother and daughter as she considered them. Instantly protective of her child, Caitlin settled her hands over Sorcha's small shoulders and drew her in close to her legs.

'Hello, Mrs MacCormac.' She forced the words out through reluctant lips, despite her vow to err on the side of optimism. 'It's been a long time.'

'It certainly has, Miss Burns.'

The other woman moved down the stone-flagged floor towards them, her hands busy removing her elegant black gloves as she did so. 'Is Flynn around? I told Bridie to let him know I was coming. I gather he was occupied when I rang earlier.'

Her implication seemed to be that Caitlin had clearly had something to do with that, and the younger woman found herself helplessly colouring. 'I'll go and tell him you're here, if you like,' she offered.

'No—wait. I think I'll take this opportunity to have a word with you first, if I may?'

'All right.' Caitlin shrugged, unable to think of an excuse to refuse, and thinking too that it was time to stop running away and instead face her fears. Perhaps lay a few ghosts too.

'And this is your child?'

'Her name is Sorcha.'

It seemed to Caitlin's sensitive hearing that Estelle was suggesting it was doubtful she could be Flynn's child too.

'Pretty little thing…lovely eyes. Hello, my dear!' She leaned forward to address the child.

Pressing closer to her mother, Sorcha stayed silent.

'I expect she's shy. Why don't we go into the drawing room? I'm sure Bridie must have a nice fire going in there.'

Wary of the unexpectedly warm manner Estelle was affecting, Caitlin tried to mentally prepare herself for the conversation that lay ahead.

'I want Bridie!'

Before Caitlin could stop her, Sorcha broke free from her mother's restraining hands and dashed down the hallway in the direction of the kitchen. In a way relieved that she had done just that—because she wouldn't want her daughter to witness any ill feeling that Estelle might extend towards her— Caitlin pushed her fingers a little anxiously through her newly washed and dried hair.

'Bridie's promised to make some buns with her,' she explained, shrugging again.

Without inviting her to follow, but somehow conveying that was precisely what she expected, Estelle turned and swept into the vestibule, then beyond into the drawing room. There was indeed a welcome fire burning in the beautiful marble fire-place, and the bright winter sun that streamed in through the Georgian windows settled on the floral and striped fabrics of the elegant furniture and soft furnishings, highlighting the faded grandeur that was so stylishly evident here and there. Flynn's housekeeper clearly took meticulous care of this grand old house, and lavished much loving attention on it.

But Caitlin very quickly turned her attention from the appearance of the room to the woman who had gone across to sit quite regally in a graceful striped armchair with a winged back.

'I don't know if you're aware, but relations between myself and my son have been under a bit of a cloud since you left these shores Miss Burns. This is the first time I've visited Flynn for at least a year, perhaps more, and the last time we met the situation was unhappily as difficult as ever. He's borne a lot of anger towards me about the way he thought I'd treated you. He partly blamed me for your leaving. That's been made clear to me on more than one occasion.'

For a moment Caitlin's heart lifted at the idea that Flynn had defended her to his mother and not entirely heaped all the blame on her.

'It must have been very difficult for Flynn all round,' she said.

Her regret was genuine. It had to have hurt him to be estranged from his family. It could only have added to his sense of isolation after what had happened with his ex-wife *and* Caitlin. However, anxious about what Estelle might say next, Caitlin elected to remain standing rather than sit down.

'I miss my son, Miss Burns. You have a child yourself…as a mother you must only want what you believe to be the best for her. Is my son the father of your daughter? Tell me the truth.'

In shock, the younger woman stared, stunned that Estelle would even consider that not to be the case after all this time. 'Yes, he is.'

'So clearly you were pregnant with her when you left?'

'That's right.'

'I thought she looked about the right age to be Flynn's child. But despite being pregnant you decided not to tell him?'

'I—I couldn't.'

'And why was that?'

Was she imagining it, or had she seen the glimmering of regret in Estelle's shrewd gaze as she regarded her? Caitlin inhaled a steadying breath.

'I heard what you said to Flynn that day, Mrs MacCormac…the day you were arguing with him about seeing me. I'd come to Oak Grove to find him, the drawing room windows were open and your voice carried clearly. I'd just been listening to my father berate me for being with him, and I was already upset and distraught. But then to hear you tell Flynn that I was only using him and would probably try to trap him with a pregnancy! How do you think that made me feel? You made a terrible judgement about me when you didn't even know me! Wasn't it enough that your son chose to be with me?'

'I interfered where I shouldn't have…I see that now. If I'm big enough to admit to making a mistake, Caitlin, are you generous enough to accept my apology?'

Surprised, Caitlin needed a moment to absorb this unexpected turn in the conversation.

'I don't believe in holding grudges. But I want you to know why I left that day. I truly feared Flynn might believe what you'd said about me. Coupled with my own doubts about how he would react at the news he was going to be a father…the only thing I could think of to do was to leave. In a million years I would never have wanted to trap him into staying with me. I loved him! It broke my heart to leave him even though I was carrying his baby at the time.'

By the time she had finished speaking Caitlin's heart was beating like thunder inside her chest.

Sighing deeply, Estelle put her hand up to her head, as if needing a moment to get her own emotions under control.

'What have you been saying to Caitlin? I hope you haven't been stirring up trouble while my back's been turned!'

Both women glanced up in shock at the tall, furious-looking figure outlined in the drawing room doorway.

CHAPTER TEN

'YOUR mother was only talking to me, Flynn.'

'That's what worries me!'

Striding into the room, Flynn glanced from what he considered to be the too-pale pallor of Caitlin's face to his mother's tightly controlled, perfectly made-up features. Frustration eddied through him. If only Bridie had told him sooner that Estelle was paying him a visit then he could have discussed it with Caitlin.

'I didn't come here to cause trouble, Flynn.' Rising to her feet, with the tight mask of her self-control slipping and distress stealing over her features instead, Estelle looked highly nervous. 'I've missed you, son, and I want to put things right between us.'

'I'll go,' Caitlin said quietly next to him, but Flynn glanced at her in alarm.

'No! Stay. This is *my* home, and if anyone's going anywhere it won't be you.'

'I'll go for a walk…give you two some time together. I'll be back, I promise.'

As her wide blue eyes met and held his, Flynn tried to quiet the small storm going on inside him. Fear of losing what he had only so recently gained was almost overwhelming.

'Don't be long,' he told her, reluctantly agreeing.

Caitlin left the house and walked into a wind that almost cut her in two. The sunlight was deceptive. The temperature could surely not be much above freezing. But right then she couldn't have cared how cold it was, because she had other, more pressing things on her mind.

It seemed as though her life had come full circle after her meeting just now with Estelle. The other woman's apology had come as a total surprise. Caitlin found herself hoping and praying that this time the outcome would be different—that she would at least have a chance to make things right with Flynn. Could she trust this new feeling of optimism that was slowly coming into being, starting to bud like a spring flower that had been lying dormant all winter, waiting for the time to blossom at last?

If she had to leave him again she didn't think she could stand it. She had been pierced to the core by the longed-for sight of him in town that day, and even then Caitlin had known that some how, some way, she had to help create another more hopeful ending to this story. And now…seeing the way he was with Sorcha—how he delighted in his little daughter as much as any doting, loving father— how could she possibly believe it right to go back to England, taking his child with her?

And yet…could Flynn love Caitlin as she longed for him to love her after all the bitterness and pain? Did he even have the ability to do that after the hurt he had suffered at the hands of his ex-wife?

Crossing her arms over her black sweater, to try and protect herself from the worst of the wind, she followed a winding gravelled path to the secluded garden at the back of the house. There was a charming old summerhouse there, she remembered, and she could take shelter inside if it wasn't locked.

Finding no barrier to her entry, Caitlin let herself inside and shut the door. With the wind howling around her—the stand of slim fir trees at the bottom of the garden was almost bent double by the force of it—she sat down in a simple chair fashioned from local rush work with a cross-stitched cushion at her back and dropped her head in her hands…

'Caitlin?'

Lost in her thoughts, it took a couple of seconds for her to raise her head at the sound of that masculine voice. Flynn stood framed in the narrow doorway, the top of his head almost reaching the lintel.

'You should come back into the house now. It's cold out here.'

'Has Estelle gone?'

'She's getting acquainted with her grand-daughter. Is that all right with you?'

'So you've made it up, then?'

Entering the light-flooded space, Flynn care-fully shut the door behind him. 'She told me you heard us arguing that day…that you heard what she said about you trying to—'

'Trap you by getting pregnant.'

Caitlin couldn't help wincing at the memory.

'No wonder you left.' As he moved to stand in front of her, Flynn's expression was painfully rue-ful. 'I made it hard for you to trust me, to tell me that you were carrying my baby, and then you heard that! Maybe I would have done the same in your shoes, if I'd been eighteen and hurt like you must have been. We all let you down, Catie…me, my family, your father…I see that now. But if I had been more willing to open up to you, to confide in and support you, it wouldn't have mattered what anyone else thought or did.'

'I never wanted to trap you into staying with me, Flynn. I only ever wanted you to be with me if you wanted that too. But I was so confused about what I thought you felt. How could I have known at the time what you'd been through? What made it so hard for you to trust?'

'I think I—'

'Mr MacCormac!'

The summerhouse door flew open and Bridie stood there, puffed and out of breath, looking as though she'd run all the way from the house.

'It's Sorcha! She took a tumble down the stairs and knocked herself out!'

'What?'

'Oh, my God!'

The three of them ran out together, Flynn grabbing Caitlin by the hand and sprinting past the housekeeper to get to the house as quickly as he could.

When they arrived in the generous-sized entrance hall, Estelle was sitting at the end of the carpeted staircase, cradling a tearful Sorcha in her arms. The child was awake and gazing around her, and Caitlin sent up a quick heartfelt prayer of thanks that she wasn't still unconscious. But she knew they weren't out of the woods yet.

'She was showing me how she could skip, and before I realised what her intention was she'd run up the steps and turned round to skip back down them. It happened in an instant. Oh God, son, I'm so sorry!'

Estelle's distress was genuine and heartfelt, her features the colour of whey.

As Bridie came back into the hall behind the little group, Flynn turned immediately to the housekeeper. 'Bridie, go and phone the doctor, will you? Tell him what's happened and ask him to come right away!'

'Yes, Mr MacCormac.'

She bustled off to do as she was bid.

'Oh, sweetheart—did you hurt yourself?' Tenderly stroking back some silky fair hair that had fallen into her daughter's eyes, Caitlin saw the egg-sized lump that was forming on her forehead as she did so. 'Mummy told you to be careful on the stairs, didn't she?' Her stomach somersaulted with the strain of the fright that had seized her.

Behind her, Flynn leant forward to carefully examine the contusion himself. 'How long was she unconscious for?' he questioned his mother.

'It can't have been much more than twenty seconds,' Estelle replied anxiously. 'She started to open her eyes just after I got to her.'

'Do you hurt anywhere else, *mo cridhe*?' His voice infinitely gentle, Flynn lifted one of Sorcha's small pale hands and held it.

She shook her head, her bottom lip quivering, trying not to cry any more. 'I hurt my head!' she told him plaintively.

'I know, angel, but you're going to be all right. The doctor is coming to take a look at you to make sure. Do you feel a little bit sick or dizzy?'

Sorcha nodded. 'A little bit sick.'

'You won't feel like that for long, I promise. We'll soon have you feeling well and comfortable again.'

Bridie appeared from the direction of the drawing room. 'Dr Ryan's on his way. He said he'll be here in about twenty minutes. You're to stay with her and make sure she doesn't try to get up until he arrives.'

'Let me take her, Mother. We'll take her into the drawing room and lay her down on the couch. Bridie…can you go upstairs and fetch a blanket?'

They all had an anxious time until the doctor arrived. Flynn sat holding Sorcha's hand, telling her stories to help distract her, while Caitlin sat at the other end of the couch, closely watching for any signs that might give further cause for concern.

After doing a fair amount of pacing and watching herself, to Caitlin's surprise Estelle went into the kitchen with Bridie, to help make them all tea, and returned with it all set out on a tray to serve it.

Dr Ryan turned out to be a very gentle, affable man—just the sort of caring professional a parent would want to tend to their hurt child—and after thoroughly examining Sorcha he took great pains to assure Caitlin and Flynn that the little girl was going to be just fine. For the next twenty-four hours they should keep an especially close eye on her, he advised, but other than that the following day she should be back to her old self.

Estelle and Bridie left them alone with their

daughter after the doctor had departed. Caitlin sat with knots in her stomach for a different reason. Flynn sat there, not saying a word, and she couldn't help but be anxious about what was going through his mind.

Sorcha's accident had shaken them all up, and there was a sense of something changing in the rhythm and shape of things that she couldn't deny. As for herself, she felt emptied and drained—as wrung out as a dishcloth. But in a strange, inexplicable way she felt cleansed too. A light had been shone into all the protected and dark corners where secrets had been hidden for too long, and the truth was at last exposed. But what Flynn intended to do about that truth, she hardly dared guess.

One thing was clear—Sorcha wouldn't be going anywhere very far without her father. Even now, her little face gazed up at him from the plumped-up pillow behind her head, as though he hung the moon and stars combined.

'Hey, there…you okay?'

His warm, vibrant tone interrupted her preoccupied thoughts, and Caitlin stared back at him for a moment, not comprehending. Every time he turned that too-striking gaze on her she experienced an answering anticipatory tug deep inside her womb. It wasn't just for Sorcha's sake she wanted to be close by.

'Better now,' she admitted, her slender shoulders drooping a little beneath her black sweater.

'Our resident ghost has more colour than you!'

'You have a *ghost*?'

'A very benign one…a lady who watches over the broken-hearted, so legend has it. Her lover was a reckless young MacCormac she'd recently married, whose sense of adventure drove him to spend a large part of his life at sea. His ship sank in a storm in the Atlantic one night long ago. She set a lantern in her bedroom window and kept watch every night, waiting for him to come home.'

'How sad! What was her name?'

'Lizzie. But enough of sad tales and family ghosts…I'm more concerned with how *you're* doing.'

'I got the fright of my life when Bridie said Sorcha had knocked herself out! I told her not to play on those stairs, but she's a mind of her own, that one.'

'How can she not, with you and I as parents?' Flynn commented wryly.

He was smiling at her just as he'd done in the old days, when they'd first been together—a smile that was a sensual threshold to the man's true beguiling nature. Feeling heat rise inside her, Caitlin knew her own smile was tinged with sudden shyness.

'Talking of ghosts…your mother didn't look too good there for a while either.'

'Yes, well…' A flash of his old resentment tightened Flynn's mouth. 'Perhaps she's finally realised it's her grandchild that almost ended up in hospital today!'

'She was as shocked as we were. You could see that. Don't be mad at her.'

'You've got a heart as wide as the ocean, Caitlin Burns!'

'What are we going to do, Flynn?' Tracing the fine intricate lacework on the cushion she held in her lap, Caitlin glanced back at him with anxiety in her eyes. 'About *us*, I mean?'

'We have to talk,' he said straight away, his expression becoming almost stern. 'But not now... Let's just see to Sorcha's needs for today, and tonight, when she's asleep in bed, we'll have every opportunity to discuss things.'

'Everything all right?'

Flynn glanced towards the door as Caitlin returned from the bedroom, where she'd gone yet again to take a peek at the sleeping child. 'She hasn't stirred since the last time we looked.'

'Good. Come and sit down before you fall down. You look barely able to stand up!'

To say he was on edge was an understatement. Concern for both his daughter *and* her mother cut deep. Sorcha had put the fear of God in him when she'd fallen down those stairs. It had hit him then how great was the responsibility of fatherhood...how strong the bonds of love that tied him to his child for ever. There would always be a place in his heart for the little boy he had lost, and he would never forget those early days when he had been a father to him, but now he knew it was his daughter who needed his love.

Now that Flynn was reassured she was all right, and was sleeping a perfectly natural sleep—not succumbing to any dangerous drowsiness that suggested her accident was the cause—he could give all his attention to Caitlin. Something he'd been craving all day. There was so much to say—but where to start?

CHAPTER ELEVEN

How did you heal a fracture that had been left untended for much too long and was so bent out of shape that perhaps there was no restoring it to its former health?

Watching Caitlin, her flawless skin far too pale against the funereal black of her sweater, Flynn determinedly fielded the deep sense of rejection that overwhelmed him when she sat on the couch at the opposite end to him. Assuming distance between each other—*any* kind of distance—should not be happening after the sensual delight of earlier today. Not after Flynn had experienced the fiercely sweet excitement of her body again, and she had matched him kiss for passionate kiss, their racing hearts beating as one.

But perhaps she wanted to put distance between them after the way he'd treated her—shutting her out as he had done. He could hardly blame her when he must have caused her untold grief with his aloof behaviour.

'I thought you might like to look at these.' She was handing him a small red photo album the size of a wallet. 'I keep these in my bag…I remembered I had them just now. There are some baby pictures in there, as well as a couple of Sorcha at one and two.'

With a tight feeling inside his chest as he took the proffered album, Flynn briefly met the serious blue eyes that tentatively locked with his. Here in the flickering firelight the colour took on the bewitching hue of a sky caught betwixt twilight and dusk. He knew only too well what looking into them did to his body…

'Thanks.'

Silently he studied the photographs, taking his time, his thoughtful sculpted profile seeming to drink in the details as though to consign them to memory for however long he lived.

As Caitlin glanced from Flynn towards the fire and back again, she reflected on the long, painful journey of 'growing up' that had culminated in her return to her homeland. Remembering her folly of once believing that falling in love should be so simple—that love could and *would* surmount any obstacle with ease—she felt as though she'd aged a hundred years since then, with all that had happened. Now, studying Flynn again, she silently conceded that the web of passion and hurt that had enmeshed them both was probably going to tighten when they started to discuss their future…a future Caitlin was by no means certain would turn out the way she longed for.

'I like this one.'

'Which one's that?'

Before she realised she'd done it, Caitlin had scooted up the couch to sit right next to Flynn, and peered over his shoulder at the particular photograph he had referred to. It was one that her aunt Marie had taken a couple of hours after Caitlin had given birth to Sorcha. She was sitting up in the hospital bed, a pink knitted shawl courtesy of her aunt draped round her shoulders, holding the baby in her arms. Her smile looked wan and tired, but somehow happy too.

Oh, how she had longed for Flynn to be there that day to see their child born! Thinking of the strange mix of elation and sadness she had experienced at that momentous time, she tried to stem the torrent of emotion that inevitably throbbed through her.

'I'm not exactly looking my best in that picture.' She made a face.

As he turned to study her, a deep furrow creased Flynn's handsome brow. 'You both look incredible. It's the most beautiful picture I ever saw,' he told her, a distinctly husky catch in his mesmerising voice.

'I wanted you to be there that day,' Caitlin confessed, her own voice barely under control. 'I couldn't sleep that night for thinking of you…even though I was exhausted.'

'I don't like to think of you in so much pain, giving birth alone,' he admitted, the palpable tension in him giving powerful weight to his heartfelt words.

'Aunt Marie waited outside, and the midwife and doctors were very kind. And it's true what they say—you forget the pain you've been in as soon as they put that baby into your arms. I remember looking down at Sorcha for that very first time, and I thought, So this is what they mean by a miracle. But actually…' She paused as she gazed into his eyes, knowing that her own were like crystalline windows, giving him access into the deepest part of her soul. It was too late to stop him from seeing inside, and much too late to hold anything back now that the floodgates were opened. 'Actually it was missing you that caused me the most pain, Flynn. It was like a part of my heart was cut out, not having you there.'

The tightly clenched jaw and self-deprecating twist of his mouth took her aback.

'I'm surprised you can still say that after all I've done!'

'What do you mean?'

'I thought I could never forgive you for walking out on me…but I've learned that it's *you* that needs to forgive *me*. All this time I wore my resentment towards you like a shield. A form of protection, I suppose…to guard against ever being so enraptured again. Instead of realising that I'd given you very little access to my true self, not enough for you to trust me, I chose to blame you for leaving.' As he closed the little wallet, his sigh was deeply regretful. 'I let what happened with Isabel make me bitter, Caitlin. So bitter that I didn't really realise how fortunate I was when you came into my life. It wasn't until after you'd left that it came to me what a gift I'd had within my grasp. The truth is I should have made a better effort to find out where you'd gone—but I let my pride stop me. Instead of licking my wounds and feeling sorry for myself I should have gone to your father and pleaded with him if need be for him to tell me where you were!'

'Ah, sure…you're not the pleading type, Flynn!' Caitlin's smile was both tender and forgiving.

Flynn caught her hand and, capturing her fingers, raised them to his lips and kissed them.

'Isabel's actions taught me to be very wary of relationships. When I met you I was terrified at how easily you could unravel me, with just the simplest of smiles. You had a way with you that could reach places inside me nobody had ever reached before. I knew you were dangerous from the very first time I saw you.'

'Dangerous?'

For a moment there was doubt on Caitlin's face.

'I know you don't have a calculating bone in your entire body, Caitlin! I don't doubt my mother knows it too now. That's not what I meant.'

His hand moved to cup her small delicate jaw. 'I meant that you were dangerous to my very heart…you couldn't help but crack it wide open.'

'And now?'

'Now we have to start to mend what was broken. I must have put you through hell! You were a young girl, alone and pregnant in a strange country, and I should have been there to help you! I want you to know that I'll always regret that. But we need to take this one step at a time, sweetheart…and I'm not saying it's going to be easy.'

Sensing the reservation in his voice, Caitlin tensed and pulled away from his tenderly stroking fingers.

'If you think it won't work…If you think we can't—'

'There's been hurt on both sides. All I'm saying is that some healing needs to take place first, before we can make a more permanent commitment to each other.'

His words made sense. There was no rushing this. They both had to be certain this was what they really wanted. There was Sorcha to think of too. They couldn't afford to make any more mistakes.

Sighing, Caitlin rested her head against the top

of Flynn's muscular arm. Carefully he moved her so that her head lay against his chest instead, his arm protectively around her shoulders.

'Tell me one of your stories, Flynn,' she entreated him softly, her eyelids fighting to stay open after the tensions and drama of the day. 'Tell me a story where everything seemed to be lost but in the end hope won the day.'

Staring into the fire, Flynn allowed himself a small, satisfied smile. Luckily for her, he knew lots of stories like that.

Their moving forms cast shadows on the wall in the dark gold lamplight of Caitlin's bedroom. Flynn's hands enclosed her hips, and she received him into her with a small breathless sigh, shutting her eyes to absorb the sensation of their two bodies now moving as one. A sense of rightness and completeness washed over her—almost a sense of being 'home' at last. That was what being there, with all the barriers down—mental, physical and spiritual—meant to Caitlin.

'Open your eyes,' he ordered softly, and she did, her gaze touching all the planes, shadows and sculpted angles of his strong long-boned face with unashamed love.

'Did you miss this?' she whispered, smiling as she adjusted her body to take him even deeper.

His eyes darkened in the lamplight, and he

released a sensuous groan that made her shiver with pleasure. It wasn't just his touch that held her spell-bound—his voice, with its rich velvet timbre, had always had the power to affect Caitlin deeply. Now his hands moved to stroke and cup her breasts, his fingers squeezing and releasing the tight aching buds of her dusky-rose nipples with increasing pressure.

Caitlin barely heard his answer to the provocative question she'd phrased because she was so swept up in the tide of soul-drenching pleasure that drowned out every other thought.

'Aye…I missed it badly. Now you're just going to have to make up to me for lost time.'

He guided her head possessively down to his, and his kiss was hot, hungry and rough with need. The tension inside Caitlin magnified and almost took her over the brink.

'I promise,' she gasped. 'If you just let me—if I could only—'

'This?' Flynn said throatily against her mouth, and thrust upwards strongly into her core, holding himself there deliberately until he sensed her tight, quivering muscles convulse around him.

Then and only then, with her soft-voiced cry echoing in his ears, did he let go of the barely leashed control he'd been holding onto with an iron will ever since Caitlin had opened herself to take him. With his body's longed-for release he spilled his hot, urgent seed inside her and kissed her again—the longer his mouth stayed in contact with hers, the more tender the kisses he wrought.

His feelings seemed to consume him and fill up every previously fiercely guarded corner of his heart. There was no other woman on God's green earth that Flynn wanted to be with but *her*. What had he been thinking about earlier when he'd suggested some healing had to take place before they could make a more permanent commitment to each other? Just being here with Caitlin and Sorcha was more than enough healing, wasn't it? It was certainly more than Flynn could ever have dreamed of having during all those long, lonely years he'd spent without her...

Caitlin had told Flynn that she was on the pill. But now—without the worry of falling pregnant, and able to make love freely without fear—she found herself idly wondering if she might ever have any more children with Flynn. Sorcha was nearly four years old, and part of Caitlin had never really wanted her to be an only child. But whatever happened she wouldn't bring another child into the world as a single parent. The years she'd raised Sorcha alone had been the toughest, most challenging years of her life. It just wouldn't be fair to visit that struggle on another child. In her opinion, if at all possible children needed both parents in their lives. Look how Sorcha had blossomed and seemed to grow more confident since she had been reunited with her father!

'What are you thinking about?' Flynn demanded gently, as he helped ease Caitlin down next to him on the bed.

'You mean you expect me to be able to *think* after that?' she laughed huskily.

To his amazement, Flynn felt himself grow achy with desire all over again. 'Tell me,' he urged, his jade eyes intense as they roved across her flushed and lovely face.

'I was wondering if we might ever have any more children together,' she admitted softly. 'I know we still have things to work out between us, but I—'

'I'd like a son.'

'What did you say?'

'I'd like a son—a brother for Sorcha.'

'You would?'

'Are you going to doubt everything I say from now until we grow old?' he asked, feigning vexation.

'Until we grow old?' Comprehension dawned, and her eyes went very bright. 'To be honest, I much prefer harmony to arguments. I grew up with enough of those between my father and me to be frankly weary of them!'

'I'm sorry that he hurt you and then you lost him.'

'He's in a better place now.' Her arm went confidently across Flynn's chest and she snuggled her body up close to his. 'With my mam.'

'Aye.' He pressed his lips against her honey-scented hair. 'And you, Caitlin? Are *you* in a better place? A place you might consider staying for some time?'

Her heart almost missing a beat, Caitlin sucked in a steadying breath. 'Oh, yes, Flynn! This is where I want to be…with you and Sorcha. Most definitely.'

'Good.'

Smiling to himself, Flynn moved his hard, muscular body carefully atop hers, sensing a thrill ripple through him at the surprise and then pleasure that registered on her face.

'Because I swear to God, I don't ever want to be without you again!'

Bridie breezed into the family dining room downstairs, where they were eating breakfast, and placed a small, somewhat tattered envelope on the table in front of Caitlin. There was no name or address on the front.

'Mary Hogan dropped by with this a few minutes ago. She wouldn't come in when I asked her. Just said to make sure that I gave this to you and to tell you that Ted McNamara found it down the side of the couch in your father's parlour.'

As Bridie caught Caitlin's eye the older woman's smile was full of her characteristic kindness, as if she'd intuited that the letter would be both a surprise and a shock to the young woman.

His handsome face wearing a frown, Flynn studied Caitlin closely as she picked up the envelope and stared at it.

Her stomach tightening with anxiety, she turned hot and cold all over. To calm her nerves, she put down the envelope and spread some marmalade on her toast, then turned briefly to smile at Sorcha. Thankfully she seemed none the worse for wear after the drama of yesterday, and even the lump on her head had gone down considerably.

'Aren't you going to open it?' Flynn asked her in surprise.

'Of course I am!'

Gathering her courage in both hands, Caitlin picked up the letter again. Sliding her finger under the barely sealed yellowed flap, she opened it and drew out the single sheet of paper that was inside. Instantly recognising her father's large spidery handwriting, she started to read the sparse contents.

Dear Caitlin

I've tried many times over the years to tell you how much I've missed you, but after your mam went it wasn't easy for me to be with you. You are so like her in so many ways that it almost hurt to look at you.

I'm sorry that you went away and that I never asked to see the child. At first I wouldn't look at the pictures you sent, but after a while

I made myself look at them. Sure, she's a grand little thing, isn't she, your Sorcha? I wish you would come home so that I could see her for myself, but if the truth be known I don't suppose I will even have the courage to send this letter. I've been very foolish, and not a good father to you, and I know your mam would wipe the floor with me if she were around!

I see that MacCormac fella around from time to time, and I'd like to tell him where you are but I don't have the heart for it. Would he have made you happy? I don't know, but I am sorry I stood in your way when you wanted to be with him.

Look after yourself, Catie—and give the little one a kiss from her grandfather.
Dad X

Hardly trusting herself to speak right then, Caitlin kept hold of the letter as the tears welled up hotly in her eyes.

'What's wrong, Mummy?' Sorcha asked, a spoonful of cereal poised in mid-air. 'You're crying!'

'Bad news?' Flynn too was staring at her, his handsome face grave with concern.

'Dad must have written this some time ago.' She wiped at a tear and made a feeble attempt at a smile. 'But he never got round to posting it.'

'Can I see?' Holding out his hand expectantly, Flynn took the scrawled page and avidly scanned it.

All this time Caitlin had believed that her father had never forgiven her for 'disappointing' him and winding up as a single mother. He'd been so hard on her, and she'd never understood why. Now, astonishingly, she'd learnt that he *had* loved her after all—but she had reminded him too much of her mother, the woman he had loved and lost too soon. And she had also discovered that he had indeed thought about his grandchild, and would have been happy to meet her. However, on the downside, it had pierced her heart to read the part about Flynn.

'What a foolish old man!' His voice gruff, Flynn leant towards Caitlin and gently touched her damp cheek with the back of his hand. 'If only he had made himself post it! Look at what he lost out on because he didn't!'

'He was afraid. After he lost my mam he was afraid of everything. His whole life was ruled by fear. I can see that now. I can see it and forgive him.'

'Like I said…' His arresting glance wry, Flynn shook his head. 'You've a heart as wide as an ocean, and I for one wouldn't have it any different!'

'It's all in the past,' she said with a determined smile. 'It's the present and the future that's the important thing…don't you think?'

'Daddy, I want to go and see the horses! Will you take me?' Sorcha glanced expectantly up at her father, milk from her cereal glistening on her small chin.

'Later, darling…I promise. But first I have to go somewhere with your mother this morning.'

His commanding glance towards Caitlin clearly denoted that he expected complete agreement with this previously undisclosed plan, and apprehension mingled with surprise inside her.

'Bridie thought you might like to go and play in the garden for a while, if you wrap up warmly,' Flynn continued. 'She might even let you plant some bulbs in your own little patch for the spring.'

'Yes, but I have to have my own shovel!' the little girl replied with relish.

The two adults laughed aloud in unison.

'What have I raised?' Shaking her head, Caitlin wiped at her mirth-filled eyes.

'In a few years she'll be running for Taoiseach, that's for sure!' Flynn grinned in agreement.

Emerging from an alley of hornbeams that in the spring would create a magical canopy of lush green growth, Flynn pulled the car up in front of an elegant Georgian country house with a graceful white-pillared portico. It was a beautiful dwelling that anyone would be proud to live in, surrounded as it was by dense woodland and verdant lawns. And because of its secluded position it was naturally very private.

'Are we visiting someone?' Twisting round in

the passenger seat to rest her gaze on her companion's implacable features, Caitlin frowned. 'I wish you'd told me! I would have dressed up a little.'

Not that she had much of a wardrobe to choose from since most of her clothes were still at home with her aunt Marie. But Caitlin would have preferred something a bit better than the habitual jeans and sweater combination she'd been wearing since she'd arrived in Ireland if she were going to be introduced to some of Flynn's friends.

'There's no need for you to dress up when there's only you and me here, *mo cridhe*.' He smiled, using a Gaelic endearment, his compelling eyes crinkling at the corners.

'I don't understand…' Shrugging with frustration, even though her heart squeezed tight at his affectionate address, Caitlin drew her dark blonde brows together in puzzlement.

'I own this house,' he explained.

'You do? It's lovely!'

'It needs a bit of a work done on it, seeing as though it's been standing empty for a while. The tenants left just before Christmas. But I won't be letting it again.'

'No?'

'No.'

Suddenly his expression was very serious.

'I'm giving it to you, Caitlin.'

'Giving it to me? How do you mean?'

'The deeds will all be in your name. It's a wedding present…so you'll never be without a place to call home again.'

It was hard to believe the evidence of her own ears. To be given a house—and a house such as this! That was amazing enough…but to be given it as a *wedding present*?

Tears swam helplessly into her eyes. 'A wedding present, you say?'

She sat quietly, her hands scrubbing at her increasingly damp cheeks, and it was Flynn who— driven past all endurance—pulled her fiercely into his arms and kissed her. When he lifted his head after doing the job more than thoroughly, he grinned at Caitlin like the cat that had got the cream.

'Can I take that as an acceptance? I should have asked you four and a half years ago, if I'd had any sense at all, but I was too damned cautious for my own good back then!'

'It's what I've always wanted…from the moment I saw you…to marry you. I *knew*…I knew even then you were the one for me.'

'It was the same for me.'

For just a moment Caitlin saw such unfettered emotion in Flynn's glance that it seemed to suggest he was on the verge of tears, and then he brushed back her hair with slightly trembling fingers and gazed at her as if it was *she* who hung the moon.

'I love you, Caitlin. I've waited a long time to tell you that.'

'I love you too, Flynn…and it's a love that will endure for ever. I have no doubt about that.'

'Well, then…this will be a new beginning for both of us. You have complete *carte blanche* as to how you do the place up, by the way. When it's been decorated to your satisfaction we'll move in here—you, me and Sorcha.'

'But what about Oak Grove?' she asked concernedly.

'I still have to help oversee the place, but my brother Daire can help with that like he's always done. He's away travelling at the moment, but when he gets back I'll put him in the picture. We'll keep my apartment there for visits—and I've got my writing retreat up in the mountains too, don't forget. But once we're married this will be our home—if you're in agreement?'

'If I'm in agreement? I'm in seventh heaven! But, as wonderful as this gift of yours is, I have to tell you that I don't mind where I live as long as I can be with you. The ancient circle of belonging can't be broken, Flynn…you of all people know that. Wherever you and me and our children are together…*that's* home.'

Laying her head against the warm, protective wall of his chest, Caitlin sighed softly as she realised with joy that this was exactly the sort of homecoming her heart had always dreamed of.

◎™ MILLS & BOON®
Pure reading pleasure

JANUARY 2008 HARDBACK TITLES

ROMANCE

The Martinez Marriage Revenge	978 0 263 20222 9
Helen Bianchin	
The Sheikh's Convenient Virgin *Trish Morey*	978 0 263 20223 6
King of the Desert, Captive Bride *Jane Porter*	978 0 263 20224 3
Spanish Billionaire, Innocent Wife *Kate Walker*	978 0 263 20225 0
His Majesty's Mistress *Robyn Donald*	978 0 263 20226 7
The Rich Man's Love-Child *Maggie Cox*	978 0 263 20227 4
Bought for the Frenchman's Pleasure	978 0 263 20228 1
Abby Green	
The Greek Tycoon's Convenient Bride	978 0 263 20229 8
Kate Hewitt	
A Royal Marriage of Convenience	978 0 263 20230 4
Marion Lennox	
The Italian Tycoon and the Nanny	978 0 263 20231 1
Rebecca Winters	
Promoted: to Wife and Mother *Jessica Hart*	978 0 263 20232 8
Falling for the Rebel Heir *Ally Blake*	978 0 263 20233 5
To Love and To Cherish *Jennie Adams*	978 0 263 20234 2
The Soldier's Homecoming *Donna Alward*	978 0 263 20235 9
The Italian Surgeon Claims His Bride	978 0 263 20236 6
Alison Roberts	
Desert Doctor, Secret Sheikh *Meredith Webber*	978 0 263 20237 3

HISTORICAL

The Dangerous Mr Ryder *Louise Allen*	978 0 263 20186 4
An Improper Aristocrat *Deb Marlowe*	978 0 263 20187 1
The Novice Bride *Carol Townend*	978 0 263 20188 8

MEDICAL™

The Surgeon's Fatherhood Surprise	978 0 263 19851 5
Jennifer Taylor	
A Wedding in Warragurra *Fiona Lowe*	978 0 263 19855 3
The Firefighter and the Single Mum *Laura Iding*	978 0 263 19859 1
The Nurse's Little Miracle *Molly Evans*	978 0 263 19863 8

◎™ MILLS & BOON®   1207 Gen Std LP

Pure reading pleasure

JANUARY 2008 LARGE PRINT TITLES

ROMANCE

Blackmailed into the Italian's Bed *Miranda Lee*	978 0 263 20010 2
The Greek Tycoon's Pregnant Wife *Anne Mather*	978 0 263 20011 9
Innocent on Her Wedding Night *Sara Craven*	978 0 263 20012 6
The Spanish Duke's Virgin Bride *Chantelle Shaw*	978 0 263 20013 3
Promoted: Nanny to Wife *Margaret Way*	978 0 263 20014 0
Needed: Her Mr Right *Barbara Hannay*	978 0 263 20015 7
Outback Boss, City Bride *Jessica Hart*	978 0 263 20016 4
The Bridal Contract *Susan Fox*	978 0 263 20017 1

HISTORICAL

A Desirable Husband *Mary Nichols*	978 0 263 20109 3
His Cinderella Bride *Annie Burrows*	978 0 263 20113 0
Tamed By the Barbarian *June Francis*	978 0 263 20117 8

MEDICAL™

Single Dad, Outback Wife *Amy Andrews*	978 0 263 19926 0
A Wedding in the Village *Abigail Gordon*	978 0 263 19927 7
In His Angel's Arms *Lynne Marshall*	978 0 263 19928 4
The French Doctor's Midwife Bride *Fiona Lowe*	978 0 263 19929 1
A Father for Her Son *Rebecca Lang*	978 0 263 19930 7
The Surgeon's Marriage Proposal *Molly Evans*	978 0 263 19931 4

◎ MILLS & BOON®
Pure reading pleasure

FEBRUARY 2008 HARDBACK TITLES

ROMANCE

The Italian Billionaire's Pregnant Bride	978 0 263 20238 0
Lynne Graham	
The Guardian's Forbidden Mistress	978 0 263 20239 7
Miranda Lee	
Secret Baby, Convenient Wife *Kim Lawrence*	978 0 263 20240 3
Caretti's Forced Bride *Jennie Lucas*	978 0 263 20241 0
The Salvatore Marriage Deal *Natalie Rivers*	978 0 263 20242 7
The British Billionaire Affair *Susanne James*	978 0 263 20243 4
One-Night Love-Child *Anne McAllister*	978 0 263 20244 1
Virgin: Wedded at the Italian's Convenience	978 0 263 20245 8
Diana Hamilton	
The Bride's Baby *Liz Fielding*	978 0 263 20246 5
Expecting a Miracle *Jackie Braun*	978 0 263 20247 2
Wedding Bells at Wandering Creek	978 0 263 20248 9
Patricia Thayer	
The Loner's Guarded Heart *Michelle Douglas*	978 0 263 20249 6
Sweetheart Lost and Found *Shirley Jump*	978 0 263 20250 2
The Single Dad's Patchwork Family	978 0 263 20251 9
Claire Baxter	
His Island Bride *Marion Lennox*	978 0 263 20252 6
Desert Prince, Expectant Mother *Olivia Gates*	978 0 263 20253 3

HISTORICAL

Lady Gwendolen Investigates *Anne Ashley*	978 0 263 20189 5
The Unknown Heir *Anne Herries*	978 0 263 20190 1
Forbidden Lord *Helen Dickson*	978 0 263 20191 8

MEDICAL™

The Doctor's Royal Love-Child *Kate Hardy*	978 0 263 19867 6
A Consultant Beyond Compare *Joanna Neil*	978 0 263 19871 3
The Surgeon Boss's Bride *Melanie Milburne*	978 0 263 19875 1
A Wife Worth Waiting For *Maggie Kingsley*	978 0 263 19879 9

MILLS & BOON® 0108 Gen Std LP

Pure reading pleasure

FEBRUARY 2008 LARGE PRINT TITLES

ROMANCE

The Greek Tycoon's Virgin Wife *Helen Bianchin*	978 0 263 20018 8
Italian Boss, Housekeeper Bride *Sharon Kendrick*	978 0 263 20019 5
Virgin Bought and Paid For *Robyn Donald*	978 0 263 20020 1
The Italian Billionaire's Secret Love-Child *Cathy Williams*	978 0 263 20021 8
The Mediterranean Rebel's Bride *Lucy Gordon*	978 0 263 20022 5
Found: Her Long-Lost Husband *Jackie Braun*	978 0 263 20023 2
The Duke's Baby *Rebecca Winters*	978 0 263 20024 9
Millionaire to the Rescue *Ally Blake*	978 0 263 20025 6

HISTORICAL

Masquerading Mistress *Sophia James*	978 0 263 20121 5
Married By Christmas *Anne Herries*	978 0 263 20125 3
Taken By the Viking *Michelle Styles*	978 0 263 20129 1

MEDICAL™

The Italian GP's Bride *Kate Hardy*	978 0 263 19932 1
The Consultant's Italian Knight *Maggie Kingsley*	978 0 263 19933 8
Her Man of Honour *Melanie Milburne*	978 0 263 19934 5
One Special Night... *Margaret McDonagh*	978 0 263 19935 2
The Doctor's Pregnancy Secret *Leah Martyn*	978 0 263 19936 9
Bride for a Single Dad *Laura Iding*	978 0 263 19937 6